THE GREAT
REMINDER

Also by Robert Irvine

THE GREAT REMINDER

R.R.

[Robert] Irvine

St. Martin's Press · New York

L-2

The author wishes to thank Stephen Jay Gould,
whose essay "Shoemaker and Morning Star" suggested the title of this book.

Design by Judith A. Stagnitto

Library of Congress Cataloging-in-Publication Data

Irvine, R. R. (Robert R.)
    The great reminder / Robert Irvine.
        p. cm.
    "A Thomas Dunne book."
    ISBN 0-312-09302-0
       1. Traveler, Moroni (Fictitious character)—
Fiction. 2. Private investigators—Utah—Salt
Lake City—Fiction. 3. Salt Lake City (Utah)—
fiction.   I. Title.
PS3559.R65G7   1993
813'.54—dc20   93-10337
                                      CIP

First Edition: July 1993

10 9 8 7 6 5 4 3 2 1

To Cynthia Merman

THE GREAT
REMINDER

ONE

As usual Brigham Young was creating a traffic jam at the head of Main Street. He'd been standing there in bronze since the horse and buggy era.

Behind Moroni Traveler someone honked repeatedly.

"Gentile!" Traveler muttered on Brigham's behalf.

Double-lane traffic had come to a standstill at the point where South Temple shrank to a single, buggy-size lane. Through it all Brigham stood his ground, looking majestic atop his granite pedestal. He'd been leaning on his cane there in the middle of Main and South Temple streets for nearly a hundred years. At his feet a bronze cast of characters—an Indian, a fur trader, and a pioneer family—kept him company.

Half a block beyond the Mormon leader, the afternoon sun was hiding behind the Chester Building, where Traveler had his office. He glanced at the dashboard clock. He was late. No doubt his prospective client was already into the Yellow Pages seeking a replacement.

Once through the intersection, Traveler parked illegally in

front of the Chester Building and climbed the three flights of stairs rather than wait for the elevator. Outside his office, a well-dressed elderly man stood hunched over an aluminum cane. When Traveler opened the door for him, the man gently tapped the rubber tip against the frosted glass panel and scowled. "It says Moroni Traveler and Son."

"My father's out of town," Traveler said.

"Then you're the one I spoke to on the phone?"

Traveler nodded at the chair on the client's side of his desk. Four feet away his father's desk had its own client's chair.

"As I informed you when I called, I'm Major Lewis Stiles, U.S. Army retired."

Long retired, Traveler thought. The man, now holding himself rigidly erect like a soldier awaiting inspection, looked eighty at least. His dark gray suit hung on him loosely. The collar of his white shirt was a size too big despite a tightly cinched regimental tie. Once seated, he balanced his metal cane squarely across his thighs before adding a timeworn, two-strap briefcase to his lap.

"When you called," Traveler prompted, "you asked for an immediate appointment."

Major Stiles's arthritic hands showed a maze of blue veins as he transferred his briefcase to the floor beside his chair. Free of it, he pointed a crooked finger at the open window behind Traveler. "I came here directly from the temple across the street."

Traveler started to swing around to join in the view of Salt Lake City's Mormon landmark, then caught himself and kept his eyes on his prospective client.

"May I ask you something personal, Mr. Traveler?"

Traveler nodded.

"Are you one of us? Are you LDS?"

"The closest I come is people threatening to baptize me when I die."

Stiles leaned back and appeared to think that over. After

a moment he sighed. "What do you think of cemeteries, Mr. Traveler?"

Traveler looked for signs of humor in the man's face but found only deep wrinkles and sad blue eyes. "I'm a private detective, not a philosopher."

Stiles pursed his lips, lurched to his feet, and hobbled across the office to the other, east-facing window. He swayed momentarily after coming to a stop. A steady breeze, warm for so late a May afternoon, came through the open window and stirred the few strands of white hair that fringed the major's head.

Traveler rose to his feet but stayed behind the desk. From there, he could see over the man's shoulder to the snow-capped Wasatch Mountains, looking coldly molten in the late afternoon sun.

"When I was your age," Stiles said, "I never thought much of cemeteries either. But each time I pass one these days, it calls out to me. 'Old man,' it says. 'Your time's up. You belong to me.' "

He thumped the floor with the tip of his cane before leaning his weight on it. "I'm glad you're not one of us, Mr. Traveler, despite being named for our angel." He nodded to himself and turned around. "I have a feeling this is a job for a Gentile, not a Saint."

Traveler settled back into his chair. Cross-ventilation brought the scent of mountain sage and juniper in from the east and out the temple-facing window. He breathed deeply and prodded the major with an encouraging smile.

"There's a time factor involved." Stiles lifted his cane until it was pointing at Traveler. Without the stick's support, he wobbled slightly. "That's why I want to get things started as soon as possible."

He peered at Traveler for a moment, then grunted as if satisfied with what he saw. "Cemeteries, Mr. Traveler. They'll get you too in the end."

"My father is a great one for pioneer graveyards."

■————————■

"Looking for relatives like the rest of us, I dare say. We do it in the daytime, though, don't we? We say to ourselves cemeteries are so beautiful and peaceful in daylight, but how they frighten us at night."

The man held up a hand to forestall comment. "My wife's buried up in City Cemetery. That's where I'll rest, too, when I'm called home. The trouble is, I can't go yet. Not without setting matters right."

Traveler adjusted the lined yellow pad in front of him but made no move to write on it.

"Right after the war, I bought side-by-side plots. A good thing, too. These days, City Cemetery's running out of room. My son and his family are going to have to find their own resting place when their time comes."

Shaking his head, Major Stiles returned to the client's chair and eased himself onto its hard wooden seat. "Listen to me, an old man rambling on like he had all the time in the world. Like I said before, Mr. Traveler, I've come to you to help set matters right before it's too late."

Grimacing, he reached into the inner pocket of his suit coat and removed an unsealed envelope. He studied it for a moment before setting it on Traveler's desk. "Go ahead. Take a look for yourself."

Inside was a cashier's check for $132.07. It was made out to Karl Falke and/or Moroni Traveler.

"That's how much I owe the man," Stiles said. "He had fourteen dollars and seventy cents coming to him back in July of 1945. That's the amount I deposited at five-percent interest. As of now, it comes to what you see there, one thirty-two oh-seven."

"Are you saying this man's been missing since 1945?"

"I know it's a long time ago, but you come highly recommended, Mr. Traveler. Someone important in the church says you're the one to get tough jobs done. Even impossible ones."

"That sounds like something Willis Tanner would say."

——■————————■——

4

"You're lucky to have a friend like that, a man who speaks for the prophet himself."

"Willis and I go back long before he was a spokesman for the church."

"Then I can't help wondering why you're not a Saint, why—" Stiles's teeth snapped together. "There I go again, wandering off the subject. It used to be that being LDS was important here in our promised land. But look at Salt Lake now. Half the people on the streets are Gentiles like you. You're driving us Saints out."

Traveler sighed. "What about this man, Falke?"

"He was a Gentile, all right. The last time I saw him he was a twenty-four-year-old German prisoner who looked older than I did, and I was thirty-nine at the time. That was back in July 1945."

That made Stiles eighty-seven, Traveler calculated.

"Karl Falke had been through a lot in the war, of course. As for me, I was too old to fight, or so said the powers that be."

Stiles expelled a deep, shuddering breath. "I was commissioned in '41, two months before Pearl Harbor. I was already thirty-five then. They wouldn't have taken me at all except for my bookkeeping background, plus a lot of ROTC I'd had in high school and college. By 1943, I was a paymaster for the German prisoner of war program here in Utah."

Traveler studied the check again. Why couldn't Karl Falke have been something simple, like a runaway wife?

"As paymaster, I was responsible for reimbursing the prisoners. Eighty cents a day we paid them for war work. That came to twenty-one dollars a month, the same pay our own soldiers were getting at the time."

Stiles leaned forward. "I can see you're wondering why enemy prisoners needed money. They had their own canteens, for one thing, where they could buy cigarettes and candy. Whatever they didn't spend, they could save. That's how Falke's fourteen dollars and seventy cents started accumulating."

"What kind of work did he do?" Traveler asked for lack of anything better.

"I'm coming to that. First, you've got to understand the times, the situation. Early in the war, our main consideration was security. POWs were kept behind barbed wire and guarded closely. Utah was a center for that. Eventually, we had more than twenty thousand prisoners in this state. It was a good place for them, too, because there aren't any international borders nearby and a hell of a lot of desert to cross if you're headed for one."

Stiles reached into his side pocket, removed a carefully ironed white handkerchief, and wiped his brow. "By 1945, things had changed. Our manpower shortage was critical. We needed help to bring in the crops. That's why we had to use POWs, by the thousands, too. Karl Falke was one of those working the sugar beet fields down south in Cowdery Junction when he disappeared."

Traveler got up to check the state map that his father kept under glass on the top of his desk. Major Stiles joined him.

"Here," Stiles said, jabbing a finger at Sevier County where the largest town has a population of fifty-four hundred. Cowdery Junction, like its nearest neighbor, Salina, had fewer than two thousand people.

"The sad thing is," Stiles went on, "Falke's disappearance came two months after Germany surrendered. The war should have been over for him."

"Tell me what happened."

"We had a big problem on our hands at that time. As a result, he wasn't the only one who tried to escape, but he was the only one who wasn't rounded up and accounted for."

Stiles returned to his chair. Traveler did the same.

"An escaped prisoner," the major continued, "was a job for the MPs, not the paymaster. But the MPs gave up the search too soon. I said so at the time. If it had been up to me, I would have kept looking."

"What makes you think the man's still alive?" Traveler asked.

"That's what I want you to find out."

When Traveler didn't respond, Stiles laid down his cane and hoisted his briefcase onto the desk. The smell of saddle soap came with it. His gnarled fingers fumbled with the buckles. By the time he had them undone, his hands were shaking badly. The color had drained from his face and he was breathing noisily through his mouth. He didn't speak again until he had himself under control.

"When the doctors told me I had cancer, I started cleaning out my trunk. I wanted to sort out the past so my son wouldn't have to do it after I'm gone. That's when I came across my old war records. Thank God I had the foresight to have some of them duplicated back in '45. Otherwise, I wouldn't have enough information to give you a fighting chance."

Traveler suppressed a groan.

"At first I told myself these old papers were nothing but mementos. But my conscience knew better. I knew I'd have to make an accounting one day. That should have been the government's job, of course, but you know bureaucrats. Instead of sending that money to Falke's wife, they took back his check, along with half a dozen others that belonged to POWs who hadn't lived to cash them. It was my own money that went into his account."

"Give it up, Major. Too much time has gone by."

Stiles shook his head. "When you get to be my age, you'll know how important time really is. You'll come to realize that the past has a way of catching up with you."

"I don't see what I can do."

Stiles dismissed the comment with a brusque, backhanded gesture. "You're too young to remember what it was like during the war. Utah's POW camps were scattered from Logan in the north to Cowdery Junction in the south. There were eleven main camps in all, plus auxiliary bivouac areas set up to cope with the manpower shortage. Take Salina, for

———•———

7

instance, where the massacre happened. Workers were as scarce as hen's teeth down there. As a result, the farmers were yelling for every POW they could get. Their sugar beets were rotting in the fields, they said. Sugar was rationed in those days, of course, and worth its weight in gold."

Stiles paused to clear his throat. He was about to continue when someone knocked softly on the door. Until then, Traveler hadn't noticed the shadow outlined on the frosted glass.

"Come in," he called.

The door opened halfway but Nephi Bates, the Chester Building's elevator operator, made no move to enter. Instead, he stood on the threshold, rocking on the balls of his feet and smiling weakly. The earphones from his cassette player were looped around his neck, muffling but not silencing the Mormon Tabernacle Choir.

"I'm sorry to intrude," he said, "but I have a message for Mr. Traveler."

"What is it?" Traveler asked.

"In private," Bates answered.

Traveler looked at Stiles, who nodded and said, "My throat could use a little rest anyway."

Traveler rose and followed Bates down the marble hallway to the grillwork elevator.

"My conscience got the better of me," Bates said as soon as he was seated on the collapsible stool inside the cage. "That man's been haunting me ever since I carried him up here to your floor."

"My clients are confidential."

"He's in pain. I could see it on his face, in the way he walked. I haven't seen suffering like that since my father died."

"He says he's ill," Traveler admitted.

"He changed when he got out of the elevator," Bates said. "His pain disappeared. He hid it away like a guilty secret."

Traveler stared at Bates. Usually the elevator operator confined his comments to Mormon scripture. Because of that, the building's owner, Barney Chester, claimed that

---

Bates was a spy for the church. Even so, he'd been working the elevator for years.

"He needs your help," Bates said.

"I'll keep that in mind," Traveler said.

Bates closed the grillwork door and replaced his earphones. "For once I hope you live up to your angel's name."

TWO

By the time Traveler reentered his one-room office, Major Lewis Stiles was standing at the window looking out at the temple.

"It's a comforting view, Mr. Traveler. I hope you realize that." With a sigh, the man settled onto the granite window-sill. "Now, let's get back to those sugar beets in Salina. Sugar was crucial to the war effort. To help the farmers bring in their harvest, we rushed in a temporary camp with tents instead of the usual wooden barracks. A couple of hundred German prisoners were sleeping in those tents one night when a guard went berserk and opened up with a machine gun. Nine POWs died. A hell of a lot more were wounded. That's history, Mr. Traveler, written down in the record books. What came later is known to only a few."

Traveler slipped into the client's chair.

"After the machine-gunning," Stiles continued, "a day didn't go by without trouble. Prisoners began sabotaging the camp. They threw everything at the guards that wasn't nailed down. Our men got even more trigger-happy. One shot himself in the leg, another fired on a prisoner he thought was escaping but who was actually on his way to chapel. One of the newspapers said we were running a death camp. That's why the other six deaths had to be hushed up."

Grunting, the major rose from the sill and faced the temple again. After a moment, he rapped a knuckle on the window glass. "Six of them were working over in Cowdery Junction. One day they were fine, the next day they took sick and died. We never did find out what killed them."

He leaned his forehead against the pane. "You have to understand, Mr. Traveler. Times were chaotic. Even though Germany had surrendered, we were still fighting a war in the Pacific."

His breath misted the glass. "Thinking back on it, maybe we should have tried harder to find out the cause of those six deaths. I'm no expert, no doctor, but we should have done something. Instead, we buried them anonymously in the cemetery at Fort Douglas."

Traveler failed to see the connection with the missing man. He was about to say so when Stiles continued. "I always thought it looked like some kind of poisoning. I'm sure others did too, though nobody was saying so out loud. You see, our German prisoners had been getting good treatment up until the end of the war. It was policy. If we treated them right, we hoped the Germans would do the same for our boys. In any case, when people found out what the Nazis had done in their death camps, attitudes changed. There were plenty of high-ranking people who thought the six dead men had it coming to them."

Stiles stepped back from the window and turned around. "My memory's not what it used to be, but I'm sure it was one week to the day after those six POWs died that Karl Falke went missing. July 1945."

Traveler reached across his desk, retrieved the yellow legal pad, and wrote the date on it.

Nodding, Stiles walked around the desk. Traveler rose and they traded positions, Stiles in the client's chair once again, Traveler behind his desk.

Stiles said, "You couldn't blame Falke for disappearing, not with the rumors going around. There was talk those six had been machine-gunned like the others. It wasn't true, of course. They just took sick, like I said. Don't think we didn't do our best to save them either. We rushed them to the local hospital. Even so, we had half a dozen escapes right after that. As I said before, though, we rounded up everybody but Falke."

"Could he have died like the others and not been found?"

"Wandered off someplace and died, you mean?" Stiles closed his eyes momentarily as if visualizing the suggestion. "We conducted an extensive manhunt and even used dogs. They're good at sniffing out bodies."

"What else can you tell me about Falke?" Traveler said.

"I have letters from his wife."

Tattered envelopes came out of the briefcase. The letters inside were written in German.

"After the war, Mrs. Falke contacted everyone she could think of. The commandant at Fort Douglas, the governor, even President Truman. Finally, when no one could help her, she settled on me. She wrote to me for years. I have stacks of letters at home somewhere. She didn't stop writing until she died a few years back."

"Did you answer her?" Traveler asked.

"Early on. I told her there was nothing I could do, that her husband was only one of hundreds I had working the farms. That didn't stop her. It hasn't stopped her from haunting me either. The Falkes had a son, a boy. He was killed in the bombings in 1944."

Carefully, the old man returned the letters to his briefcase. "I have translations somewhere, though I haven't been able to put my hands on them. I don't think they'd help you anyway. They were mostly about her loneliness."

Stiles straightened his shoulders. "What do you say, Mr.

Traveler? Don't you think it's time you went to work? The cemeteries are filling up. Soon there won't be anybody left who remembers what happened, or even cares about it."

Traveler glanced at his father's vacant desk. If Martin were here, he could play the heavy and turn down the case. Traveler sighed. He knew his father would do no such thing.

Traveler made a stab at rejection. "My father's the expert on missing persons."

"When I spoke to Willis Tanner, he told me your father was due back in town tonight."

"My father chooses his own cases."

"I've anticipated your reluctance," Stiles said, "thanks to our Mr. Tanner."

"What has Willis been saying?"

"That you and your father aren't the kind of men who give up easily."

"Take my advice," Traveler said. "Save your money."

"Falke was one of the few prisoners we had in Cowdery Junction who could speak passable English. That would have helped him survive in the countryside."

Traveler thought that over. "Do you think it's possible that he could be passing himself off as an American?"

Shrugging, the major reached into his coat and came out with a stack of hundred-dollar bills. Licking his finger, he began counting them out on Traveler's desk.

"Did Willis tell you to bring cash?"

"A man in my position, expecting to be called home any moment, wants everything settled up front. I don't want to leave the dirty work to my heirs."

"I don't like to commit my father without consulting him," Traveler said.

Stiles leaned forward and stared him in the eye. "I don't need Willis Tanner to tell me you're a man I can trust. Both of you, you and your father, are named for our angel."

"My father prefers to be called Martin."

"Why Moroni Traveler and Son on the door, then?"

"His train arrives early in the morning," Traveler said.

"Knowing Martin, he'll be in the office first thing. You can ask him yourself tomorrow."

Stiles smiled, fished a document from his briefcase, and handed it to Traveler. It was a government form. *Basic Personnel Record (Alien Enemy or Prisoner of War)* was printed across the top. The date, *11 June 1943,* was printed in the bottom left-hand corner.

Attached to the form were two photographs, front and side views of Karl Falke, plus fingerprints and a description. He was twenty-two years old at the time the form was filled out, five feet ten inches tall, weight 160, blue eyes, medium skin color, and brown hair.

"That was issued two years before his disappearance," Stiles said.

"He wouldn't look like this anymore."

"I'm ahead of you there. My son followed in my footsteps. He's a bird colonel in the Pentagon. When I told him I was going after Falke, he did some research for me and came up with the name Otto Klebe. I don't remember him personally, but according to records in Washington, he was a prisoner at Cowdery Junction the same time as Karl Falke. After the war, Klebe returned to this country and settled in right here in Utah. Brigham City to be exact."

Leaning heavily on his cane, Major Stiles started to rise. Halfway up, pain overwhelmed him. His face crumpled. He caught his breath and dropped the cane. By the time Traveler retrieved it, Stiles's pain had disappeared, wiped clean by a self-control that left Traveler in awe.

"They tell me I have a month at the most," Stiles said. "I'd like to have this business settled before then, before I'm called home. What do you say, Moroni Traveler? Are you with me?"

"There's little chance of finding someone after so many years."

"But you'll look, you and your father. You'll send me home having tried at least."

Traveler took a deep breath and nodded.

"By God, Willis Tanner was right about you." Stiles handed Traveler a calling card. "If you're quick enough, young man, you'll be able to reach me at that number."

■——————■

THREE

The Denver and Rio Grande Railroad Depot, built in 1910, was showing its age. Its terra-cotta brick had lost its luster; its white marble had grayed; its immense arched windows looked black instead of the green glass Traveler knew them to be. The vaulted, Renaissance Revival waiting room had been turned into a museum, while passengers were relegated to an Amtrak annex filled with plastic chairs and vending machines. Yet somehow the smell of cigars and brass cuspidors that Traveler remembered from his childhood lingered.

He checked the arrival board. The 4:00 A.M. train from Los Angeles, via Milford, Utah—on time when Traveler had phoned fifteen minutes ago—was now scheduled to arrive at 5:30 in the morning.

With nearly two hours to kill, he eyed the dozen or so West Temple winos spread out among the synthetic chairs. Rather than intrude, he was about to go searching for a coffee shop when the men's room door swung open. Out came Mad Bill, Salt Lake's Sandwich Prophet, with his disciple, Charlie

Redwine, right behind him. With them came the clinging aroma of what Charlie called Navajo tobacco. Smoking it in Utah was both a sin and a felony. Seeing the pair so early in the morning probably meant they'd been up all night.

A nearby wino raised his head, sniffed the air, and slid out of his chair. His panhandling fingers were reaching for Traveler when Charlie shouted at him in Navajo. The man stopped and turned to face the Indian.

"Private preserve," Bill translated as soon as he moved between Traveler and the panhandler.

Bill was a big man, well over six feet, almost as tall as Traveler, though a lot softer. Even so, the panhandler shrugged and retreated.

Charlie muttered more Navajo.

"He says to tell you, Moroni, that donating to our cause is a good investment. You can think of it as insurance."

Bill had exchanged his usual prophet's robes and proselytizing sandwich boards for creased tan slacks and a pressed shirt. Charlie's jeans looked new, his cowboy boots spit-cleaned.

"How much insurance do I need?" Traveler asked.

"The Church of the True Prophet is always grateful for contributions of any size." A smile made the Sandwich Prophet wince and touch his swollen cheek.

"Haven't you seen the dentist yet?" Traveler asked.

It was Charlie who shook his head.

"I told Doc Ellsworth to expect you," Traveler said.

"Charlie's medicine keeps the pain in check," Bill replied.

"You'll be doing me a favor," Traveler said. "The doc owes me. Besides, you don't want to fool with an impacted wisdom tooth."

"I do God's work, Moroni. *He* will provide."

Traveler shrugged, knowing when to give up. "You're going to need more painkiller, then, because we've got a long time to wait for Amtrak."

The Indian reached into the neck of his shirt and extracted a full medicine bag.

■———————■

Bill touched the leather pouch and nodded. "The wait is worth it. After all, how often does a man like you find out whether he's a father or not?"

Traveler groaned inwardly. "We don't know if the boy exists. Even if he does, he's not mine."

"Don't be selfish," Bill said. "You're not the only one with a vested interest in Moroni Traveler the Third."

Charlie pointed at the waiting room clock.

"That's right," Bill said. "We're expecting another interested party any minute."

"Who else have you invited?" Traveler asked.

Instead of answering, Bill grabbed Traveler's arm and led him outside onto the floodlit sidewalk. Yesterday's smell of spring had been erased by a west wind carrying the sulfuric aroma of the Great Salt Lake.

"I was hoping for a quiet reunion with my father," Traveler said.

"We're all family," Bill answered.

Charlie gestured dramatically before folding his arms over his chest.

"Charlie says Moroni the Third will be our son, too. He says he'll teach the boy magic."

"What he's going to need is a mother," Traveler said.

"Lael is too young for you," Bill responded.

"Is that who you invited?"

As if on cue, Lael Woolley's red BMW came roaring down Third South, followed closely by another car. She feinted at the stop sign before skidding into the parking lot next to Traveler's ten-year-old pickup truck, a loaner while his Ford was being overhauled. As she threw open the door, headlights from the second car illuminated her face. In the glare, her skin looked dead white, her lipstick as black as her eyes.

"That car's church security," Bill said before Traveler could get the words out of his mouth.

The unmarked gray sedan came to a stop three rows away and switched to high beams. Lael climbed out of the BMW, shielding her eyes. She was wearing stretch jeans and a baggy BYU sweatshirt that came halfway down her thighs.

The sedan cut its engine but not its lights. Doors opened. Two men got out, one on either side, but stayed where they were, anonymous silhouettes behind the high beams.

Lael shouted at them. "I want some privacy!"

The security men got back into their car. After a moment, they doused the lights but left the doors open.

With an angry gesture, she waved them away.

"You're wasting your time," Traveler said. "You're the only grandniece Elton Woolley has."

"You'd think I could outrun them in a BMW, wouldn't you?"

"The FBI trains them well."

She stood on tiptoe to kiss his cheek and whisper, "You could run them off if you wanted to." She smelled of vanilla extract, which she used instead of perfume, along with almond and cinnamon.

"What good would that do?"

"Are you afraid of my uncle?"

Traveler tried to picture Elton Woolley. His image merged with those who had preceded him—Joseph Smith, Brigham Young, and a century and a half of successors. According to Mormon scripture, each was the direct descendant of Jesus, each a living prophet on earth.

"In this state," Bill said, "everyone answers to your uncle. Senators, congressmen, the governor, all but me and Charlie."

"What about Moroni?" she said.

"He's named for an angel. That gives him a special dispensation."

Lael smiled. "And me?"

"We're all afraid of you," Bill said.

She looked up at Traveler. "What do my Moronis say to that?"

"I'll let my father answer that when he gets here."

"I've got a long wait then. His train isn't due until five-thirty."

"See what I mean?" Bill said. "The Woolley family's sources of information, both secular and otherwise, are beyond us."

"Why are you here so early, then?" Traveler asked her.

She tugged at her sweatshirt until it was tight against her body. Beneath the garment, her stomach swelled slightly. The rest of her looked thin and fragile. "I thought it would give us a chance to talk, Moroni, about your son and my interest in him."

"I don't have a son."

Her bony shoulders rose and fell as quickly as a twitch. "His name is Moroni Traveler the Third in any case."

"Moroni isn't an easy name to live with. My father gave it up years ago."

"Uncle Elton thinks of him as Moroni." Lael rested a hand on Traveler's arm. "You saved my life, Moroni. I want to pay you back some way."

"I was working for your uncle. It was a job. He paid me."

"I spent my own money, not my uncle's, to find the boy."

Lael had paid a woman named Stacie Breen for the location of Moroni Traveler the Third. The boy, according to the Breen woman, had been sold to adoptive parents in Milford, Utah, by Traveler's former girlfriend, Claire.

Lael took a step in the direction of the depot door.

"You don't want to go in there," Bill said. "It's full of street people."

Charlie made a sign.

"That's right," Bill interpreted. "We're street people, too, but only when wearing our boards."

Traveler shook his head. "Let's find some place to have coffee. The Snappy Service over on State Street is open all night."

"There's no need," Lael said. "I've brought something hot to drink with me. It's in the BMW."

Bill retrieved a large Thermos and a stack of plastic cups from the front seat, then locked arms with Charlie to block the depot's door.

"We can't allow the prophet's kin inside a place like this," Bill said.

Lael whirled around to face the parking lot. She snapped her fingers at the unmarked sedan, pointed at the depot door, and gestured like an umpire calling someone out.

Traveler said, "Those men inside are homeless. They have nowhere else to go."

When the two security men reached her, she told them, "Give everyone inside five dollars. Then make sure they go somewhere else for breakfast."

Within a couple of minutes, the waiting room was empty. Four chairs had been wiped off and arranged in a circle so that Lael could serve their drinks.

Traveler took a sip of something that tasted like coffee-flavored Ovaltine. "Tell your uncle for me, you're not the one who needs protecting anymore."

Charlie snorted and began doctoring his Ovaltine from the medicine bag around his neck.

Seeing Lael's frown, Bill said, "It's his religion."

"Yours too, I think."

Grimacing, the Sandwich Prophet touched his swollen cheek and held his cup out to Charlie. "Medicinal purposes only, I assure you."

Lael turned her attention to Traveler. "It would have been faster if your father had driven to Milford."

"Trains remind him of his youth."

"I've never been on one," she said, looking around the waiting room with obvious distaste.

"My mother took me on the train when I was a boy. To this day, it still stops in Milford on its way to the Coast."

"What were you like then?"

Instead of answering, Traveler closed his eyes and felt his mother's hand close on his as she dragged him along to

Zion's Bank to clean out Martin's savings. Once that was done, she never let go of Traveler, not until they were on the train.

You won't miss your friends, she'd told him then. *When we get to Los Angeles, there'll be oranges to pick from our trees and sunshine to play in every day. I'll get a good job and meet the right kind of man and you'll grow up to be rich and famous.*

He'd never seen an orange tree, and Kary had never gotten a job. When the money ran out, they came back to Salt Lake to live with Martin again. After that, she pretended the trip to the Coast had been nothing but a vacation all along. The second time she rushed Traveler off to California, he ran away.

Lael said, "What about it, Moroni? Were you a Saint when you were a boy?"

"My mother never thought so."

"My uncle says I can never marry anyone but a Saint in good standing."

Bill began stroking his prophet-length beard like a man contemplating a shave.

"Saints marry in the temple and are sealed together for eternity," she added.

With a grunt, Charlie got up from his chair and began pulling handles and pushing buttons on the vending machines, chanting under his breath as if pleading with the gods to give him something for nothing.

"Have you thought of converting?" Bill said.

"To your church?" Lael asked.

"The right woman might make me convert," Bill answered. Behind him, Charlie pounded on a machine.

"Moroni Traveler the Third needs baptizing and a mother," she said.

"My father says he'll remarry if he has to," Traveler said. "For the boy's sake."

"It's you I'm talking about, Moroni. You must do the right thing by *your* son."

"Claire filed the paternity suit against Martin."

■——————■

22

Lael shook her head. "Willis Tanner has told me all about you and your family. He says he was your best friend when you were growing up."

"That poses an interesting theological question," Bill said. "Can a Gentile and a Saint be best friends? Perhaps I should make it the subject of one of my sermons."

"Try it out on me," Lael told him.

Traveler handed her his cup of Ovaltine and stood up. "I'm going for a walk."

"A sermon might do you some good."

"He's a lost cause," Bill said.

"The book says, 'Blessed are the Gentiles,' " Lael said. " 'If they repent they shall be saved.' "

Traveler walked away without comment. He kept moving, circling the block, until a loudspeaker announced the train's arrival at 5:30.

FOUR

Traveler's father got off the train looking rumpled. He glanced around the nearly deserted station platform and shook his head.

"There used to be redcaps everywhere," he said, handing his bag to Traveler. "Taxis were lined up halfway around the block. They'd practically fight to get hold of your luggage."

With a sigh, Martin moved around Traveler to greet Lael. When he stepped back from her embrace, his head was shaking again. "I'm afraid it was a waste of your money, young lady. There was no sign of the boy. No Moroni the Third, and no one who'd ever heard of Claire Bennion."

"Did you look everywhere?"

"There aren't more than fifteen hundred people in Milford. I checked with the sheriff, the local bishop, and the tithing office. I even walked through the cemetery."

Lael caught her breath. "Do you think he's dead?"

"Pioneer graveyards are a hobby of mine. Tombstones tell you a lot about people, no matter how long they've been dead." Martin rubbed his eyes and sighed. "One thing's for sure. There are no Travelers planted in Milford and no Bennions either. I checked for Bennions in case Claire used her own name instead of Moroni's."

Lael bit her lip. Bill reached out to comfort her, but she stepped away.

Martin grabbed Bill's outstretched hand and shook it as if it had been intended for him all along. "Look at you, Bill. No sandwich boards, no robes. You too, Charlie, dressed to the teeth." He shook hands with the Indian. "I wasn't expecting a reception committee."

"I paid that Breen woman a lot of money," Lael complained.

A timer clicked somewhere and the depot's outside security lights went out, even though the rising sun was still behind the Wasatch Mountains.

Martin said, "Tell us again what Miz Breen told you about Milford."

" 'It's a small town,' she said. 'The kind of place to raise children.' " Lael shivered in the chill air and pulled her hands up inside the sleeves of her baggy sweatshirt. "Over and over, she kept saying that she was Claire's best friend. That she knew how Claire thought."

Traveler shook his head. That wasn't the Claire he remembered. When he'd lived with her, she'd never spoken of women as friends, only rivals.

"How definite was she about Milford?" Martin asked.

"Claire never came out and pinpointed it, if that's what you mean. But it was Stacie's best guess."

"You told us you paid for solid information."

"Would you have gone looking for the boy if I'd said anything else?"

Bill moved to Lael's side. "Don't blame her. Claire's your responsibility, not Lael's."

"What the hell," Martin said. "I would have gone anyway just to see the tombstones."

He pulled a notebook from the pocket of his corduroy jacket and turned to a dogeared page. "I found an old

25

favorite. 'Behold my friends as you pass by / As you are now so once was I / As I am now, so you must be / Prepare for death and follow me.' "

Lael shrugged. "Stacie gave me a number where I could reach her in California."

"If you call her," Traveler said, "she'll want more money."

"Don't you think it would be worth it, to have another chance at finding your son?"

"We can talk about that later," Martin said. "Right now, I want *my* son to drive me to the office, so I can type out my notes on the cemetery while they're still fresh in my mind."

As soon as Traveler and his father were seated in the loaner truck, Martin leaned back and expelled a ragged breath. "God, I had a hard time sleeping on that train. It's not like the old days when the Union Pacific ran the *City of Los Angeles.* Do you remember that from the time you and your mother rode the streamliner to the Coast?"

"Vaguely."

Martin jabbed a finger in the direction of Lael's BMW, which was leaving the parking lot with Bill and Charlie on board and the church security sedan in pursuit. "Considering our success with women, take my advice, Mo, and watch out for that young lady."

Traveler eased the truck out of the parking lot and turned north on Fifth West, heading toward South Temple Street.

"She's after you," Martin said after a block. "I hope you realize that."

"Do you think she lied about Milford?"

"If I'd found the boy, she wouldn't have a reason to hang around you anymore, now would she? Not unless you married her."

"We're not even sure there is a Moroni the Third," Traveler said.

"But we keep looking, don't we?"

■――――■

"Maybe now's the time to stop."

"I want the boy," Martin said.

Traveler took his foot off the gas and coasted to the curb. "Isn't one son living at home enough?"

"A man needs children."

"Are you talking about me or you?" Traveler said.

"You spend a lifetime accumulating answers. It's all for nothing if you don't pass them on to someone."

"Don't I count?"

"Two chances are better than one," Martin said.

"We'll keep looking, then."

"We never had a choice. Claire knew that."

"I'll drive you home so you can get some sleep."

"What about you?" Martin asked.

"I have work to do," Traveler said. "A missing person."

"You can tell me about it when we get to the office."

FIVE

Traveler parked in front of the Chester Building just as the sun cleared the Wasatch Mountains. Despite the early hour, Barney Chester was at his cigar stand reading a paper, an unlit cheroot clamped between his teeth. When he saw Traveler and Martin enter the lobby, he thrust his stogie into the perpetual flame. A haze of smoke surrounded him by the time they reached the glass counter, where bags of Bull Durham, Sen-Sen, and the same ancient Chiclets had been on display for as long as Traveler could remember.

"I would have met you at the station," Chester said around his cigar, "but I figured there was a crowd already. Besides, I knew you'd need a cup of coffee this time of the morning."

"My train was due at four," Martin said. "I hope you haven't been waiting here that long?"

Shrugging, Chester grabbed the metal coffee pot from the hot plate and began filling a line of Styrofoam cups already arranged along the countertop.

"I only count the three of us," Traveler said.

"Bill and Charlie are in the men's room."

"And Lael?"

Chester jerked a thumb toward the wooden phone booth next to the restrooms. "She said something about making a call to the Coast."

Martin raised an eyebrow at his son. "Where do you think Stacie Breen will send us next?"

"Wherever Lael wants, probably."

Chester took the cigar out of his mouth and focused on it intently. "I'm sorry you didn't find the boy. I was looking forward to being a godfather."

The phone booth's door folded open with a thump. Lael waved and headed for them, her low heels echoing across the marble floor. When she reached them, she made a face at Chester's cigar. He immediately craned his head and blew smoke rings at the ceiling where a frescoed Brigham Young was leading a wagon train of pioneers to the promised land.

"Stacie Breen says she's got some other leads," Lael announced. "She'll get back to me."

"In the meantime," Martin said, "we're going to take our coffee upstairs and do some work that'll pay the rent."

She smiled. "Barney showed me how to work the elevator. I'll run you up."

Traveler glared at Chester, who said, "She's prettier than Nephi Bates."

"Talk about spies for the church," Martin said. "But I'm too tired to climb three flights of stairs."

Humming "Material Girl," she ferried them to the top floor. She didn't speak until they'd exited the elevator. "Don't worry. I'll find Moroni Traveler the Third."

The brass cage dropped out of sight before Traveler could think of a response.

"Our record with women continues to be perfect," Martin said as he unlocked the office door.

"Lael was business," Traveler said. "I didn't pick her."

■——————■

"Sure."

"How do you say no to the prophet when his grandniece has been kidnapped?"

With a sigh, Martin took up residency behind his desk. "Tell me about our missing person."

By the time Traveler finished recounting the details of Major Stiles and the missing prisoner of war, Martin was shaking his head. "Rule one: Don't mess with the church. Rule two: Don't take on hopeless causes."

"Check the petty cash," Traveler said.

Martin opened the bottom drawer of his desk and took out the metal box. "Rule number three: Never take money from old men who are dying."

"If you'd been here, you wouldn't have been able to turn him down either. He says he can't die happy unless we clear his conscience of Karl Falke."

"Have you considered the odds? The man's been missing for more than forty-five years."

"I've run off half a dozen copies of the form with Falke's photograph."

"I can hardly wait to start passing them out."

"I've also put an ad in the *Tribune,* offering a reward."

"Perfect. All we've got to do is sit here by the phone and wait for an informant."

"You can't fool me," Traveler said.

"All right. I admit it's a challenge." Martin rubbed his hands together. "Where do you want to start?"

"You track down that ex-POW, Otto Klebe, the one who's supposed to be living in Brigham City. I'll check out Fort Douglas."

SIX

After breakfast, Traveler drove up South Temple Street toward the Wasatch Mountains. By the time he reached the entrance to Fort Douglas, he was high enough on the east bench to view the Great Salt Lake without smelling it. The water's surface, even in bright sunlight, looked as dull as a dead man's eye.

He refocused on the high ground that federal troops had commandeered in 1862. At the time, they claimed they were there to protect the overland mail routes. In reality, their orders were to keep an eye on the Mormons, who were threatening rebellion if the federal government outlawed their God-given polygamy. With that in mind, all cannons had been trained on a single target, Brigham Young's home in downtown Salt Lake.

From where Traveler had parked in front of the fort's museum, hitting such a target looked like a longer shot than his missing person. He got out of the car and went to work.

The museum building, like nearby Officers' Row, dated from the 1880s and had been built in that ubiquitous two-story military style known as Quartermaster Victorian. As soon as he crossed the threshold, Traveler was overwhelmed by the army's all-purpose smell of musty canvas. The room itself, large and barrackslike, was filled with rows of glass-topped display cases. Mannequins wearing two centuries of battle dress lined the walls. One of them, a soldier from the Revolutionary War, stood next to a wooden desk. The real man behind the desk was wearing a summer uniform of suntan slacks and shirt, though his only insignia was a plastic badge that labeled him as EARL LOCKHART, CURATOR.

Traveler introduced himself.

"I saw you play football once," Lockhart said, shaking hands, making a contest out of it. He was a compact man, somewhere in his fifties and half a foot shorter than Traveler's six three.

"I've been retired a long time," Traveler said.

"I know how you feel. You're looking at a master sergeant, U.S. Army retired." Lockhart grinned and cracked a knuckle. "You don't shake hands like someone named for an angel."

Traveler handed him a business card.

"That's more like it. A detective I can believe. Now what can I do for you?"

Traveler told him about the missing prisoner of war.

"You'll want to see our permanent exhibit, then."

They left the main museum and toured two side-by-side rooms, one for each world war. In both rooms, grainy photographic blowups covered the walls with the anguished faces of German prisoners. Traveler looked for the missing man, Karl Falke. What he found were young men with haunted eyes, none of whom reminded him of the photograph supplied by Major Stiles.

"I was a prisoner myself," Lockhart said, nodding at the soldiers on the wall.

"Vietnam?"

"We didn't bury our dead in 'Nam, you know. We brought them home." Lockhart slowly shook his head. "We still have twenty-one German prisoners in our cemetery here."

"I'd like to take a look," Traveler said.

"If it had been me, I'd have wanted to be buried at home." Lockhart hung a sign on the museum door that said BACK IN 15 MINUTES. "It's a short walk." He fell into cadence step beside Traveler.

From a block away, rows of plain white tombstones gleamed in the spring sunshine. The smell of cut grass mixed with sage coming off the mountains.

"We had twenty-three thousand prisoners in Utah during World War Two," Lockhart said. "That comes to one prisoner for every twenty-six residents at the time."

"How many escaped?"

"The twenty-one who are buried here died of natural causes, if that's what you're getting at."

Traveler shrugged without breaking step.

"When a private detective shows up talking about a forty-eight-year-old war," Lockhart said, "I can't help wondering about his motives."

They left the path and crossed freshly mown grass to a cluster of graves. The Germans had been buried together. Twenty of them had white headstones exactly like those of the American dead. One marker was made of dark granite and decorated with a chiseled swastika.

Traveler knelt down as if to examine the emblem. "I've been told there are six more German graves around here somewhere. The ones who died in Cowdery Junction."

"So that's it. I knew you were up to something. There aren't many people who know about the Junction dead. I wouldn't myself if I hadn't had the time to read every record in my own museum."

Lockhart led Traveler to another part of the cemetery where a single white stone stood alone on a piece of land big enough for six graves.

"The marker was added long after the war," Lockhart said. "Sometime in the fifties, I think, though there's nothing

33

written down about that. But that's when this entire section was planted."

The inscription on the stone read: HERE LIE SIX SOLDIERS WHO DIED FOR THEIR COUNTRY. A potted geranium stood beside the marker.

Lockhart nudged the potted plant gently with his toe. "Until three years ago, someone used to bring flowers here once a month, regular as clockwork. Then suddenly they stopped. I've got the duty now." His shoulders rose briefly. "Someone had to keep up the tradition, one soldier to another, if you know what I mean."

"Tell me about the deaths in Cowdery Junction."

"There's no secret about their names, even though they're not on the stone."

"Is one of them Karl Falke?"

Lockhart shook his head. "You're welcome to check the list back at my office. There are photostats of death certificates to go along with them. They all died of heart failure. There's also a transport document authorizing shipment of the bodies from the hospital in Salina to the cemetery here."

"What else can you tell me?"

"As a historian, you'd expect me to have all the answers, wouldn't you? Well, let me tell you, it ain't that easy. Working for the army, I have to go through channels. Considering the red tape I've run into, you'd think Cowdery Junction was classified top secret. Hell, I've gotten more information out of the ghost stories the old-timers tell around here than I have from the Pentagon."

"I'm not asking for a sworn affidavit, just a little help."

Lockhart sighed. "The scuttlebutt I get is this. Life was pretty damned good for the German prisoners here in Utah in '44 and '45. The fact is, the army was swamped with complaints from the locals, who claimed the prisoners were eating better than they were.

"Everything changed when the war ended in Europe and word got out about the atrocities. After that, people wanted revenge. The army wanted it, too, I guess, because prisoner

———•———

34

rations were cut and all privileges taken away. When those six died down south in Cowdery Junction, nobody gave much of a damn. Some say they were murdered, maybe even lynched by locals who'd lost sons in the war."

"Those death certificates you mentioned, did they say anything about autopsies?"

Lockhart shook his head. "We're talking rumors and gossip here. Most likely, those six died just the way the paperwork says. Their hearts were worn out by war."

"Is there anyone else around who could help me?"

"My predecessor at the museum is long gone, pensioned out and buried somewhere in the East. As for the old stories I heard, most of them came from the cemetery's caretaker, name of Jacob Decker. He's retired now and lives at the old folks' place on Twelfth East."

"I know it," Traveler said. "The Phoebe Clinton Home."

"That's it. I used to drop by there regularly the first couple of years." Lockhart sighed. "Since then, I've kind of neglected the old guy. When you see him, tell him I'm keeping an eye on his graves, will you?"

SEVEN

Traveler found Jacob Decker basking in a metal lawn chair on one of the sleeping porches that ran across the second story of the Phoebe Clinton Home. Decker had the warm sunlit end of the porch to himself, while a dozen or so other residents, mostly women, clustered forty feet away in the shade.

"Look at 'em," Decker said as soon as Traveler introduced himself. "They're worried about age spots and skin cancer."

His bare arms, as dark as old wood, had no more meat than a mummy's. The thick lenses of his glasses were smudged so badly his blue eyes looked milky.

"I worked outside most of my eighty years," he went on, "and I'm in better shape than ninety percent of the old geezers in here. The old crones, too." His breath smelled faintly of tobacco.

"Earl Lockhart up at the fort suggested I come see you. He says hello."

"You tell him for me, a man shouldn't have to retire, not if he's still fit."

"He gave me a message. He says he's keeping an eye on your graves."

"Did he say graves or grave?"

"Graves, plural."

Decker shook his head sharply. "You wouldn't think a man my age would love a cemetery, would you?"

Traveler shrugged.

"The secret is, young fella, you've got to love your work. Take this place, for instance. They've got a gardener around here who's never heard of a rake. No siree. He uses one of them gasoline power blowers. It's a wonder we're not all deaf from the racket. And what a stink. When he fires it up, it's like sucking on an exhaust pipe if you're out here on the porch at the time. Imagine what it must do to the flowers. They need to breathe, too, you know. Come on. I'll show you how a real gardener works."

Decker got to his feet and crossed the porch. He moved at a kind of trot, leaning forward on the balls of his feet as if seeking downhill momentum.

"Keep close," he told Traveler. "They've added so many rooms this place is like a rabbit warren. You get lost in here, you end up like the rest of us. Old and ready to blow away."

Traveler followed him down a back stairway, along a narrow corridor, through a laundry room, and finally out a back door that faced a neglected yard.

"Look there," Decker said, pointing to flower beds over-run with weeds. "Mr. Leaf-blower planted tulips, but didn't know enough to feed them, not that that would do much with the little sun they get out here."

He moved off again, following a cracked concrete path around the side of the house. Leggy tulips and paperwhites were blooming in a narrow strip of soil between the path and the wall of the house.

"Who do you think planted these?" Decker tapped himself on the side of the head. "Me, by God. I don't need a blower to keep my beds clean either."

Squatting, he gathered up some fallen leaves and tucked

them into his shirt pocket. "For Christ's sake, don't just stand there. Help a man up." He held out his hand.

As soon as Traveler hauled Decker to his feet, the old man was off again. He didn't stop until he reached a circular bed of carefully tended paperwhites that surrounded a weeping mulberry tree at the front of the house.

"Look at this place." Decker gestured at the Phoebe Clinton. "It would look deserted without me to keep things growing."

The retirement home, three stories in the center with two-story wings on either side, had been built in the 1880s by one of Utah's silver kings. It was said to be a replica of a stately home he'd once visited in England, though Traveler had his doubts. The architecture was pure Utah Gothic, right down to the massive Egyptian columns that held up an elaborately corniced, gargoyle-friezed porte cochere.

"I haven't thanked you yet, have I?" Decker said. "Your arrival saved me from naptime, young man." He wet his fingers to rub his glasses. The spit added to the murk on the lenses. "Naps are for children, which is the way they treat us around here. 'Eat your lunch, dearie, and then tuck yourself in.' That's all I ever hear. It's better to walk off a meal, I say. What do you think?"

The moment Traveler nodded agreement, Decker started his downhill gait again. He didn't slow until the Phoebe Clinton was half a block behind them.

"Walking this city is a revelation, young man. It's seven blocks to a mile, precisely. That's the way Brigham Young laid it out. Shall we try for one of the prophet's miles?"

"I'll keep up with you," Traveler said.

"Just so we're away from all the ladies who have nothing better to do than listen in on what a man has to say. Now tell me, Moroni. Why come looking for an old fart like me?"

"I'm working for a man named Lewis Stiles. Major Stiles."

"I remember him. An important officer up at the fort

during the war. He was in charge of payroll or something like that."

"You have a good memory."

Decker stopped abruptly and grabbed Traveler's arm. "My God. I know why you're here now. My prayers have been answered. That's it, isn't it?"

Moisture added a sparkle to the old man's eyes. "I've been writing letters for so many years now, I'd almost given up." He held up two bony fingers, a V for victory sign. "I've mailed off two letters so far this year. I even had the last one typed by a lady friend at the home. That's what did it, isn't it? They thought I was somebody because the letter was typed and looked official."

Traveler sighed. "Major Stiles is looking for a man named Karl Falke."

"Forty years I've been thinking about this, knowing where I wanted to rest. It goes all the way back to when I started caretaking at the cemetery. I was thirty-eight then. I guess you think that's strange, a man getting attached to the dead, but they're all the family I've got."

"Do you recognize the name Falke?"

Decker dug a finger into one ear. "I must of missed something."

"I'm trying to trace a German prisoner of war. A man named Karl Falke who disappeared in 1945."

"Then you're not here about my resting place?"

Traveler shook his head.

"Those damned bureaucrats in Washington. I've lost count of how many times I've written them. I don't think it's too much to ask, not after the years I put in. Summer evenings I'd work until dark up at the cemetery. On my own time, too. I never asked for overtime. I never expected it."

Decker turned away to wipe his eyes. "I don't mean to get blubbery on you. It's not like living at the Phoebe Clinton isn't okay, if you know what I mean. The way I see it though, it's just temporary, like waiting for a bus. When it comes time to be called home, I want to rest with my friends."

The old man started walking again, only this time he moved on his heels as if trudging uphill. "For a while there, right after I retired, Sergeant Lockhart used to come regular and drive me up to visit my boys. Lately, though, he's been too busy. Of course, things being what they are these days, what with the military cutting back, it's not a good idea for a man to take too much time off from his job. You don't want them thinking they don't need you."

He coughed, rattling like a longtime smoker. "These days, I only get to my cemetery when someone from the home's driving up that way."

"Maybe I can stop by now and then."

"Now that I think about it, Falke's not in my cemetery. Not that I know the names of my German family to say out loud, but I trimmed around those headstones long enough to know Falke wasn't among them."

"Have you ever heard the name before? Maybe in connection with a missing prisoner."

Decker shook his head. "My wife was cremated, you know. Now there's no place to go to visit with her."

"Do you remember anything about Cowdery Junction?"

The old man shrugged but his eyes gave him away.

"It's all right," Traveler said. "It's not a secret anymore."

"That's easy for you to say, but I was told to keep quiet about it."

"It's been too long to make any difference."

"Maybe you're right. Maybe I've been a fool for keeping quiet all these years." He blew out a long, noisy breath. "I always figured it would hurt my chances with Washington if I blabbed."

He reached out and laid a hand on Traveler's arm. "There are some things you don't want to go messing with, young fella."

"I won't quote you, if that's what's bothering you."

"Let's sit down and take a load off."

■————————■

Decker left the sidewalk to sit on the curb. Traveler settled beside him.

"Cemeteries are like confessionals," Decker said after a while. "You'd be surprised what people say there. They talk to the dead in front of the likes of me, a caretaker, as if I was as mute as a tombstone. I've heard it all, sex and sin."

His voice dropped to a murmur. "Once I heard that the Mormon church was to blame for what happened in Cowdery Junction. Another one of its Mountain Meadow Massacres."

Traveler swallowed a groan. More than a hundred years had passed since Brigham Young's avenging angels had dressed up as Indians to wipe out a wagon train of Gentiles, and people were still whispering about it as though it had happened yesterday.

Decker snorted. "You think I'm gaga, don't you?"

Traveler answered with a shake of his head.

"I just wanted to see where you stood, what with you being named after an angel and all. I made that massacre bit up, but I did talk to a couple of weird Germans once."

Decker grinned, showing tobacco-stained teeth. "You wouldn't have a cigarette, would you? Or better yet, a chew?"

"Sorry."

"The Phoebe Clinton isn't LDS, but they're down on tobacco just as bad. For my own good, they say. I say, I kept a pinch in my cheek for forty years and it didn't hurt me."

Decker tried to spit but couldn't raise enough juice. "Like I was saying, a couple of Germans showed up at my cemetery after the war. Sometime in the fifties, I think it was. They were nice and respectful, not so pushy like most Krauts. Not tourists either. They'd been prisoners, all right. They still had that lost look about them."

Traveler nodded to keep him going.

"They got to talking and one of them said he was sleeping in a tent down in Salina when that guard opened up. Do you know about that?"

"The machine-gunning, you mean?"

"You're damn right. My Kraut said he got shot in the stomach. It's hard to say whether it was true or not, what with the way people exaggerate their war stories and their suffering. You're too young to remember, but the camps were damned nice. Those prisoners ate as well as I did, I can tell you. Better maybe. Us locals had a name for them camps. Fritz Ritzes, we called them."

He licked his lips as if savoring the taste of a memory. "I wasn't a caretaker in those days. I was an army guard at the POW stockade in Brigham City."

He paused to adjust his glasses. "Because of my eyes, I was unfit for overseas duty. That's why they made me a guard. That put me in with a bunch of misfits, I can tell you. Your average guard was only one cut above a four-effer. Thank God none of them ever got buried in my cemetery."

Decker stopped speaking to look Traveler in the eye.

Traveler said, "Somebody's been putting flowers on the Cowdery Junction grave for years."

"They started showing up about twenty, twenty-five years back," Decker said, "before Earl Lockhart's time even. These days, of course, he does the honors."

"Who brought them?"

"A woman." Decker closed his eyes and squinted at the memory. "She was in bad health there at the last. I always figured something must've happened to her. Otherwise, the flowers would have kept coming."

He reached out to Traveler. "Thinking back on it, my health's just as bad now." He sighed deeply. "Maybe we'd better start back."

He needed Traveler's help on the return trip.

"We had to shoot the camp dogs," the old man said abruptly when they reached the home. "They said we had to do it because the prisoners were using them to smuggle in cigarettes. I buried the animals myself. After that, pets were banned, but the cigarette trade didn't stop. The other guards were making too much money on it, what with smokes and black-market food. The Germans were great ones for eating,

---

you know. We used to have a saying in the guard towers—'A German with a fork is more dangerous than an Italian with a machine gun.' "

Decker ran out of breath and didn't speak again until they were back on the sleeping porch and he was stretched out in his chair. "Come to think of it, that wounded German told me he was applying for citizenship. He said he owed his life to this country. If he hadn't been captured by us, the Russians would have killed him, he said."

"Do you remember his name?"

"I don't think he told me. Probably I didn't ask."

"Do you remember anything else?"

"He said he would have died if it hadn't been for the good nursing he got at the hospital down in Salina. 'One day,' he said, 'I intend to go back there and repay their kindness.' "

Decker winked. "Funny how some things stick with your memory, isn't it? I remember thinking at the time that he'd probably fallen for one of the nurses."

The old man sighed. "That's it, young fella. You've sucked me dry. There's nothing left to tell."

Traveler shook his hand.

"One last thing," Decker said. "If you get the chance, put in a word for me with the government. Tell them I'm going to be needing my plot up at Fort Douglas pretty soon now."

EIGHT

Traveler honked at Brigham Young. The prophet ignored him. So did traffic at the head of Main Street.

The signal light changed to green. Half a dozen cars managed to edge past the prophet before time ran out.

Resigned, Traveler counted those still ahead of him. Two lights to go, maybe three if an engine died or a driver wasn't paying attention.

He yawned. His eyes felt full of grit. Without thinking, he rubbed them. Smelter fallout from Kennecott Copper permeating the air started tears flowing hard enough to blur his vision. He gripped the steering wheel with both hands to keep from scratching. He closed his eyes. The the driver behind him honked. Others took up the call.

Blinking cleared his sight enough to allow him to ease the truck forward at the next change of light. As he did so, he had the urge to abandon the damn thing right there in the intersection. Just open the door, step out, and join the bronze figures at the base of Brigham's statue. *Whatever happened to Moroni Traveler? He had himself bronzed like baby shoes.*

Two traffic signals later, Traveler ran the yellow light, circled the block, and parked in front of Thomas's Indian Trading Post, two doors down from the Chester Building. As soon as he stepped onto the sidewalk, Bill and Charlie rushed to meet him, rattling their donation cans in his face. The placard on Bill's sandwich board read: GOD IS ALWAYS WATCHING, SO GIVE TILL IT HURTS.

"You're a godsend," Bill said. "It's been a slow day."

"How much do you need?" Traveler asked.

Bill rapped a knuckle against his board. "We got so desperate, Charlie tried one of his medicine dances but it raised small change only."

Traveler was about to ask for an encore when the Indian dashed after two ladies who'd just left the nearby Mormon Handicraft Shop. The women, looking intimidated, fed coins into his coffee can. As soon as Charlie stopped rattling his container, they fled toward Main Street, casting furtive looks over their shoulders to make sure he wasn't following them. The Indian waved them out of sight before trotting back to place the donations in Bill's outstretched hand.

Bill closed his fingers around the coins and shook his head. "We're still a long way short."

"What's going on?" Traveler asked.

Bill touched his swollen cheek.

"I told you before," Traveler said, "Doc Ellsworth won't charge you a cent. If you don't believe me, I'll drive you there myself."

"Charlie's been treating me with a dash of magic added to either Thunderbird or Wild Irish Rose," Bill said. "It makes the stuff taste as good as a California cabernet."

Traveler rubbed his eyes. "You look worse than ever."

"If I pray harder and do more magic, Charlie says the pain will go away altogether. It's a matter of faith."

Traveler hefted Bill's Folgers can. "It feels heavy enough for two or three jugs of Thunderbird."

"The poor box is not for drink alone," Bill said.

■——————■

45

Traveler handed back the can, took out his wallet, and removed a five-dollar bill.

"We've asked Lael out to dinner," Bill said.

"No Dee's burgers for her," Charlie added.

Traveler donated twenty to their cause while wondering who else but Dee's would allow the likes of Bill and Charlie inside. Then again, the presence of the prophet's grandniece would insure entrance anywhere.

"Is my father upstairs?" Traveler asked.

"He says you're supposed to pick him up for an early dinner."

Bill glanced at Charlie. The Indian folded his arms and nodded.

"You're welcome to join us and Lael at dinner," Bill said.

"Don't look so worried. She's all yours."

"Now, Moroni."

"You can tell me all about it in the morning." Traveler pushed through the revolving door into the Chester Building. He bypassed the cigar counter where Barney Chester had customers and went directly to the elevator. Nephi Bates was sitting inside on his retractable seat. His eyes were closed, his earphones in place, his cassette player on his lap.

Traveler's 220 pounds rocked the elevator.

Bates opened his eyes and held out a plastic cassette holder labeled *The Spoken Word: The Book of Mormon on Tape.*

Traveler pointed up. Bates shook his head and stared at the floor as if expecting the pits of hell to open up. When nothing happened, he slid off his seat and pushed the start lever. The elevator shuddered. Somewhere above them cables clattered in the shaft. The cage lurched upward.

Smiling, Bates nodded at the voices inside his head all the way to the third floor, where Martin was waiting in the hallway.

"I saw you talking to Bill and Charlie from the window," Martin said the moment the elevator sank out of sight.

"They're taking Lael out to dinner."

"How much did you give them?" Martin asked.

"Twenty."

"Add that to my twenty and they ought to have quite a meal."

"Did you have any luck tracking down our prisoner of war?"

"I got through to Otto Klebe on the phone. He's in Brigham City all right."

Rather than discuss details in the hall, Traveler led the way to the office, where they first checked the street below. Bill and Charlie had moved across the asphalt to panhandle in front of the temple gate.

With a sigh, Martin sank into his chair and put his feet up. "Klebe told me he didn't remember our prisoner of war."

"You sound like you didn't believe him."

"It's hard to read someone on the phone. I like looking him in the eye. Still, it seems unlikely that he'd forget the one and only prisoner in his camp who went permanently missing. Especially since Cowdery Junction was one of the smaller stockades."

"We'll have to talk to him in person."

"Not so fast. Klebe went into the electronics business after the war and struck it rich. He's Nauvoo Techtronics, the largest employer in Brigham City."

"So?"

"You haven't heard the rest of it. He joined the church and you know how Mormons love successful businessmen. He's a member of the Council of Seventy."

"We still need to see him," Traveler said.

"Are you listening to me? You've got the prophet at the top, then the Twelve Apostles, then the Council of Seventy. You know the rules. In this state, the church is a six-hundred-pound gorilla. You don't mess with it."

"So we'll be careful."

Martin groaned. "Ten minutes after I hung up on Klebe, Willis Tanner was on the phone asking for you."

"Did he mention Klebe?"

Martin shook his head. "Willis may work for the prophet,

he may even speak for the prophet, but I haven't trusted that boy since the day I caught the two of you in the basement with cigarettes and girly magazines."

"I would have bought them myself if I'd known where to go."

"That's the trouble with Willis. He always knew the angles. Now call him back and find out what's on his mind."

"I'm not up to it at the moment," Traveler said. "Let's have dinner first."

They left the office and rang for the elevator. For once Nephi Bates didn't keep them waiting. The grillwork door opened within seconds, and Bates announced, "I have a message for Moroni."

Traveler and Martin stepped inside.

"You're to call Willis Tanner," Bates said during the descent. "At once."

At ground level he settled onto his stool instead of opening the door. "This is my elevator," he said. "I take good care of it."

"No one's disputing that," Martin told him.

"Someone's been running it when I'm off duty."

"People still have to get where they're going."

"I'm here first thing in the morning and don't leave until dark."

"Barney runs us up to the third floor once in a while," Martin admitted.

"I smelled something strange on my starter's handle, like vanilla extract."

"Lael Woolley's perfume," Traveler said.

Bates's eyes widened at the mention of the prophet's grandniece; he slid off his stool and backed against the rear wall of the cage.

"Don't worry about Willis Tanner," Martin told him. "I'll make sure my son calls him after dinner."

NINE

Traveler and his father were halfway through their spaghetti at the Rotisserie Inn when Willis Tanner joined them. Judging from his blue suit, starched white shirt, and dark maroon tie, he'd come directly from his office in the old Hotel Utah building. The prophet's penthouse was there, too, atop what was once the finest hotel in the West.

"We didn't tell Nephi Bates where we were going," Martin complained.

"You've been eating here for forty years," Tanner said, looking around the long, narrow dining room with its dark wood wainscoting, white tablecloths, and trademark red water pitchers.

"Not on any kind of schedule, I haven't."

Tanner raised an eyebrow. "A man in my position has to know things."

"Are you having us watched?"

"Why would I do something like that? It would be an invasion of privacy, maybe even harassment."

"I telephoned Otto Klebe." Martin's shoulders rose and fell abruptly. "That's all."

"We can't have you annoying a member of the Council of Seventy."

"Did he complain about me?" Martin asked.

Instead of answering, Tanner picked up a menu and read the restaurant's motto. "East or West, at Rotisserie Inn, you are served the best."

Martin said, "I spoke to *Mr.* Klebe about a prisoner of war he once knew in southern Utah during World War Two. That's ancient history. So why should he sic you on us?"

Shaking his head, Tanner signaled for a waitress. When she arrived, he ordered a glass of milk and a cheese sandwich. He waited until she was out of earshot before replying. "Part of my job is to head off bad publicity. To that end, high-ranking members of the church contact me all the time. It's their duty."

"The missing man was a German soldier, not a Mormon," Traveler said. "He was assigned to the stockade in Cowdery Junction along with Klebe."

"Brother Klebe," Tanner amended. "Besides, what good can come of raking up old tragedies after so many years?"

"Who said anything about a tragedy?"

Tanner ran a hand over the top of his crew cut. "People don't hire private detectives for the fun of it."

"I promise you, this has nothing to do with the church," Traveler said.

"Everything that happens in this state concerns us."

"We'll keep that in mind."

"We can't afford to have those rumors starting up again," Tanner said.

Martin pointed a fork at him. "What the hell are you talking about, Willis?"

"I've studied my history. I know about the shooting in Salina and about those unexplained deaths in Cowdery Junction right after V-E Day."

His cheese sandwich arrived, along with lettuce, pickles, bell peppers, olives, and relish. He pushed the trimmings aside. "You can't blame people for hating the Germans during the war."

"Who's talking about blame?" Martin said.

Tanner concentrated on his sandwich, speaking only after he'd washed down the last bite with milk. "Considering the atrocities the Germans committed, it's a miracle more prisoners weren't killed. So you can forget all that talk about murder. It was never proved and even if it had been, it would have been justified."

"Thank you, Willis," Traveler said. "We didn't know there was a murder involved."

Tanner closed one eye, a sure sign his nervous tic was about to act up. "It was a rumor only. There was nothing to it. That's why I'm here."

"Relax," Traveler said. "All we want to do is help an old man who's about to die. We're not in the business of starting new rumors or adding to old ones. We're not going to hassle a member of the Council of Seventy. All we want is an interview with the man. Talking to us may refresh old memories."

Tanner turned his open eye on Martin. "What happens if I don't help you?"

Martin grinned maliciously.

"Just don't get the prophet's grandniece involved."

"Lael's got nothing to do with this," Traveler said.

"Then why is she hanging around your office all the time?"

"What do you want us to do, throw her out?"

"I hear she's going out to dinner with Mad Bill and that Indian."

"Why worry?" Traveler said. "Church security follows her everywhere she goes."

"Thanks to me, it does. Otherwise, I wouldn't know what the hell was going on."

TEN

The next morning, Martin insisted on leaving for Brigham City at dawn. That way, they'd have time to visit a pioneer graveyard he'd heard about from Miles Beecham, an old friend who was also a Mormon historian. To get there, they exited I-15 north of Ogden, turned east on State 39 into the Wasatch Mountains, then north again at Huntsville, climbing steadily on Highway 165. Forty miles later, at an altitude of nearly six thousand feet, Martin parked his Jeep Cherokee next to a dilapidated sign that said PARADISE, UTAH, AHEAD.

"It's best to walk from here," he said.

Traveler looked both ways along the mountain highway. There was nothing to see but spring wildflowers and a forest of pinyon pines. The sun wasn't high enough to ease the morning chill.

"Brigham Young sent people up here in 1863 to grow flax," Martin said. "After a few years, the winters did them in. The last survivors had to abandon everything, including their graveyard."

Martin began walking north, counting his paces from the

sign. When he reached a hundred, he turned onto a narrow footpath leading northeast.

"How far is it?" Traveler asked. Stinging nettle was everywhere and dew was soaking his trouser legs.

"About half a mile."

They went single file with Martin leading the way.

"What are we looking for this time?" Traveler asked.

"The same as always. Undiscovered Travelers."

"The church has them all on computer in the genealogy library."

"It's our duty to be certain. Only last year I turned up a Traveler in Huntsville that nobody knew about."

"The church hasn't verified him yet."

The pines gave way to a small stand of red cedars. Beyond them, the ground leveled out to reveal a graveyard. Stone piles marked some resting places. Of the dozen or so surviving wooden markers, most were children. One of them said, simply, BECKY, TWO MONTHS, GONE TO BE AN ANGEL.

"She had no last name," Martin said when they got back to the car. "She could have been a Traveler."

"It's not likely."

"I want people to know where I am."

"I'll see to it," Traveler said.

"You and the boy can come visit me."

"He'll be grown up long before you're gone."

"We've got to find him, you know. He has to know about his past."

Traveler sighed. "I'll drive."

"Do you still have that poem your grandfather wrote for you when you were a child?" Martin asked.

"I suppose it's around the house somewhere."

They both knew that Traveler had the original copy locked away in his safe deposit box at Zion's Bank.

Martin took a deep breath before reciting:

■──────■

"Are you planning so soon to climb the hill
To reach for the moon and stars?
Is the future calling my baby boy
away from his blocks and his cars?

"Won't you stay but a little while
Just as you are, my son?
Is the road so long, the years so short,
That you feel you have to run?"

Martin paused. "There's more."

"I'm listening."

Shaking his head, Martin consulted the map on which he kept track of graveyards visited. "It's faster to keep going north and then double back on Highway Ninety-one."

Traveler followed his father's directions, north through Avon and Paradise, east at Hyrum, then south again at Wellsville. Despite the backtracking, they reached Brigham City in time for their 10:00 A.M. appointment with Otto Klebe, who lived in an expensive development on the east side of town, an area that had been peach orchards when Traveler was a boy. Where roadside fruit stands once stood, there were now well-watered lawns and winding driveways.

At the end of one such driveway, Klebe stood waiting in front of a massive two-story brick colonial. He was a big man, Traveler's size, with a deeply lined face and large hands that gripped Traveler's with authority.

"I'm usually the first man in at Techtronics," he announced in a voice that had lost all trace of Germany. "Work keeps me fit, so I decided to do some yard work before you got here. That's the only way to keep the Jap gardeners honest."

The house was surrounded by an acre of lawn worthy of a golf course.

"We could have met at your office," Traveler said.

Klebe moved onto the veranda, where he kicked off his

dirty boots next to a rough hemp mat. "I don't believe in mixing business with my personal life."

He turned his back, bracing himself against the brick wall to shed his overalls. Beneath them he was wearing a bright red sweatsuit. He left the overalls where they'd fallen and led the way into a two-story entrance hall that culminated in an impressive double-winged staircase where a woman was polishing one of the gleaming oak banisters.

"Norma," Klebe called to her, "come here and meet our guests."

She wiped her hands on her apron before greeting them. "My husband's already had his breakfast, but I could fix you something if you'd like."

"These are the gentlemen Willis Tanner called about. You remember. They're both named for our angel, Moroni Traveler and son. I'm sure they've already eaten."

His wife lowered her eyes and began tucking stray gray hairs into the bun at the back of her head.

"My wife was born into the church," Klebe went on. "As for me, I had the good fortune to find God's word after the war. We're both sealed now, though, aren't we, dear?"

"Married in the temple for time and eternity," she agreed without looking up.

Traveler had the impression she wasn't pleased about the prospect, Mormon dogma or not.

"Please, gentlemen," Klebe said, "come into the living room and sit down."

Double oak doors, as highly polished as the banisters, opened onto a room a good forty feet long and thirty feet wide. It was carpeted in rose chenille and furnished with sofas and chairs that looked as if they'd never been used. Traveler's mother had spent her life trying for such an effect, to the point of covering everything in plastic, but had never succeeded.

Klebe settled onto a gold brocade sofa in front of a green marble fireplace. His wife stood behind him, her head bowed as if she were studying the top of her husband's head. Traveler and Martin took up flanking positions on white satin wing chairs.

"Those are our children," Klebe said, indicating the silver-framed photographs that ran the length of the marble mantel.

Dutifully, Traveler and his father got up again to examine the offspring, two boys and three girls.

"The boys are in the business with me. Vice-presidents already."

"And your daughters?" Traveler asked, as was expected of him.

"Still having daughters of their own, which makes us grandparents ten times over."

His wife shook her head slowly. "What's a woman to do with all those souls waiting in heaven to be born? The children have to keep coming."

"Don't start," Klebe said.

She backed away from the sofa. "We must accommodate the waiting souls, the spirit children. It would be a sin to do otherwise."

"Mother, these gentlemen aren't here to discuss theology. They have a schedule to keep. So do I."

"I'll be in the kitchen," she said and left the room.

Klebe rubbed his hands together. "Now, what can I do for you?"

"As I told you when I called," Martin said, "we're trying to locate a missing prisoner of war, a fellow German named Karl Falke."

"I misled you on the phone. The name only came back to me after I started thinking about the war again."

Klebe shook his head as if surprised at his own memories. "I was taken prisoner in Africa and held in the desert for quite some time before being shipped to Boston. The whole time, in the desert and on the boat, I kept thinking I was going to be tortured and killed. That's what we were told to expect if we let ourselves be captured. The fact is, I ate better as a prisoner than I ever did as a German soldier.''

He laced his hands behind his head and leaned back against the immaculate sofa. ''When we docked in Boston, we were told to think of ourselves as guests of the United States government. Imagine that. What came next is even more incredible. Instead of loading us into boxcars the way soldiers traveled in Germany, we were put aboard Pullman coaches.

''We couldn't believe it. We thought it propaganda at first. That we'd soon fall on hard times. But they never came. Even when we reached our permanent camp in Tremonton, up the road from where we sit here in Brigham City, they continued to treat us well. They gave us new uniforms and three meals a day.''

He smiled. ''I probably wouldn't have survived the war if I hadn't been captured by the Americans.''

''What about Karl Falke?'' Traveler prompted.

''We must have met when they sent us to Cowdery Junction, where we were needed for the sugar beet harvest.''

''What was life there like?'' Traveler said.

''Damned hard work, I can tell you. We were in the fields by dawn and didn't leave again till dusk. We each had a quota, half an acre of sugar beets, thinned and weeded. Without us prisoners, your farmers wouldn't have gotten their crop in that year.''

Klebe shook his head. ''Hitler told us we'd be in the United States by 1945, but he didn't say anything about sugar beets.''

Klebe stood; his hands went to the small of his back. ''What I remember most was the constant backache from stooping over in the fields. The pain was always with us and we were always exhausted. The weather was a killer, too, that summer. Over a hundred degrees for days at a time. Naturally, the farmers knew better than to work out in that kind of sun, but we didn't have the option. Some of the locals were kind, though. They felt sorry for us and brought cold milk and homemade bread. God, I remember how good that tasted, not like the stuff you buy in stores today."

He moved to the fireplace and leaned his back against a hearth that showed no soot. For the first time, Traveler realized the house was cool, probably not much higher than the sixty-degree temperature outside.

"One of the farmers said we Germans worked harder than their Mexicans. I know for sure we did twice the work the Italians did. Hell sakes, the farmers wanted us to stay on through the 1946 harvest. You couldn't blame them, since their own sons weren't back from the war yet."

He stared at one of the silver frames for a moment. "Do you like old photographs?" he asked Traveler.

"My father collects them."

"It's an old man's hobby, all right. It's how I finally placed Karl Falke in my mind, through some old camp photos. He wasn't actually in them, but his face came back to me just the same. He was older than I was by several years. I don't think we spoke more than a few times. Of course, I was a lowly *Fusilier,* a private. Falke was a *Sanitatsunterfeldwebel.* That's a sergeant in the medical corps. I have a vague memory that he grew up on a farm and that his family was ambitious enough to send him away to the university before the war. As for me, the army grabbed me the day I turned seventeen."

"So you're saying you weren't a friend of his?" Traveler asked.

"In those days, you had to be damned careful who you picked for a friend. There were Nazis in camp, hard-liners, who kept order and took down names for reprisal after the war."

"Was Falke a Nazi?"

Klebe shrugged. "Weren't we all? Still, who can remember that long ago? It's been nearly half a century, and there aren't that many of us left alive. One thing's for sure. It was never a good idea to commit yourself one way or the other."

"What were your politics then?" Traveler asked.

"I was a patriot. Who isn't at that age? I'd been indoctrinated, for God's sake. I'd been told Germany would win the war. We all thought we'd be marching up Pennsylvania Avenue one day just like Hitler promised."

"What did Falke think?" Martin said.

"Like I told you, he was older. He probably knew better. I did, too, by 1945. That's when I fell in love with this country. I vowed I'd return after the war was over and find myself a wife. By God, I did, too."

Klebe snatched up one of the framed photographs and thrust it at Traveler. It showed a woman in coveralls with her hair tied back with a bandanna. "That's my Norma working for the war effort. She was a patriot, too, one of those Rosie the Riveters in a defense plant."

"Let's get back to the Nazis," Traveler said. "Did they ever do anything more drastic than take down names?"

"I told you before. I was young. I don't think the noncoms trusted me." He turned away to replace his wife's photograph. "I *do* remember when Falke went missing. There'd been several unexplained deaths around that time. Most of us in camp blamed the Americans, though some thought the Nazis were settling old scores while there was still time."

"Are you saying he was murdered?" Martin asked.

"It's possible."

Martin shook his head. "How would they have hidden the body?"

"We were doing farm work at the time. The guards weren't with us every minute. The way I figure it, a group of prisoners working together could have buried someone in one of those beet fields."

Martin ran a finger around the helix of his ear. "Tell us more about Falke's background."

"I have the impression that he came from Munich. But I can't be sure after all these years. Like I said, we weren't close."

"Can you think of anything else that might help us?" Martin asked.

Klebe started to shake his head, then turned the gesture into a nod. "Come to think of it, you might want to talk to my brother-in-law, Grant Hansen. He was an American officer at the camp. Naturally, your army used only the dregs to man their POW camps. Men who weren't fit for anything else. Even so, you might get something out of the old boy."

"Where can we find him?" Martin said.

"My brother-in-law works for me now, at my subsidiary plant in Kearns. He's past retirement age, but I keep him on for sentimental reasons." Klebe smiled. "You know how it is."

Traveler guessed Klebe to be a good five years beyond retirement himself.

"I came to this country with nothing," Klebe added. "Look at me now. You see before you one German who won the war."

As Traveler rose to leave, he saw Norma Klebe standing in the doorway. The look on her face said her war was far from over.

ELEVEN

The Idle Isle Cafe on Brigham City's Main Street had been a tradition since Traveler was a boy. Each time he returned to the small town, he held his breath, expecting change.

A sigh of relief escaped him as he crossed the threshold. The marble soda fountain was still intact, the homemade candy still on display in old-fashioned glass cases.

Martin grunted appreciatively as he swung onto the counter stool next to his son. They both ordered the same thing they'd been having for decades, hamburgers and chocolate egg malts. By the time they topped off the meal by splitting a piece of homemade pie, a light spring rain was falling.

On the drive back, the rain followed them as far as Bountiful. After that, it was sunshine all the way to the Chester Building.

Barney Chester was waiting for them just inside the bronze, art deco revolving door. He plucked Traveler by the sleeve and tugged him across the lobby to the relative privacy of the cigar stand. Martin followed.

Once behind the counter, Chester glanced toward the elevator where Nephi Bates was lost to everything but the cassette-driven sound inside his earphones.

"Bill's been arrested," Chester whispered.

"What for?" Traveler said.

"He calls it tithing." Chester's voice had risen back to normal but Bates didn't seem to be paying any attention. "But it's still shoplifting."

"We gave him plenty of money."

Chester stuck a cigar between his teeth but didn't light it. "I heard Charlie say something about renting tuxedos for the night."

"There's no problem, then," Martin said. "Bill can plead insanity and get away with it."

"Where was Bill tithing?" Traveler asked.

"The usual," Chester said. "The Era Antiques."

"I've got a deal with the owner," Traveler said. "I pick up the tab after each of their pilgrimages."

"Lael's involved this time," Martin said. "That changes the rules."

Chester thrust his cigar into the eternal flame and blew smoke toward the ceiling fresco.

"I warned you about that woman," Martin said. "I—"

A cracking sound in the lobby interrupted him. A moment later, Charlie Redwine came trotting around the corner. A hunk of his plywood sandwich board was missing.

"I got caught in the swinging door," he said. He ran a palm over his proclamation, which remained intact: GOD SAVE OUR PROPHET.

"Tell us about Bill," Traveler said.

Charlie slipped his head out of the harness and leaned the board against the cigar counter. Without being asked, Chester filled a cup with coffee and handed it to the Indian, who added a sprinkle from his medicine bag. He held the cup under his nose and breathed deeply.

"My prophet is being persecuted for his vision. He always

knew it would come to this, that they would find some way to crucify him." For Charlie, it was a long speech.

"The Era Antiques never complained before," Traveler said.

"The church is behind it."

"What did Bill steal?" Martin asked.

The Navajo tilted his head and drained his coffee. "An old piece of crockery, nothing worth getting excited about. A posy pot, Bill called it."

"I don't think so," Chester put in. "They've set bail at twenty-five thousand dollars."

Traveler started to reach for Charlie, then thought better of it. "I gave you money for Lael's dinner last night."

Charlie touched the medicine bag beneath his shirt. "She has gone to her uncle for bail."

"I don't think the prophet will get involved."

"If one prophet refuses to save another, that's proof of conspiracy." Charlie folded his arms over his chest.

"We'll have to come up with the money," Martin said. "Either that or leave Bill in the can."

Chester grimaced. "My vacancy rate is high enough as it is without word getting around that I'm financing criminals. The next thing you know, I'll have bail bondsmen wanting to open up shop here. I can see their neon signs now." Chester waved his cigar. "Thieves and cutthroats apply here."

Traveler laid a hand on his father's shoulder. "We've got twenty-five hundred in the kitty upstairs. That's ten percent, enough for a bond."

"We've spent a little," Martin said.

"Christ!" Chester handed over his wallet.

"You and Martin go get Bill," Traveler said. "I'll talk to the man at Era Antiques."

Rather than move the Jeep, Traveler decided to walk, north past Brigham Young's statue, then south on State

Street. At 251, the sign said ERA ANTIQUES SINCE 1924. The owner, Garner Davis, was a big man, nearly Traveler's size, and somewhere in his thirties. When he saw Traveler looking at the sign, he said, "My father sold his first antique back in '24. He didn't actually have a shop at the time, but that's how far back we go."

"You must know why I'm here," Traveler said.

"I tried to get hold of you before I called the police."

"I was out of town most of the day."

Davis removed a painting from the seat of a worn velvet Victorian chair. "The legs are a little wobbly, but it ought to hold you."

Once Traveler was settled, Davis moved behind an inlaid walnut desk piled with reference books and receipts.

"I know you've made good for Bill in the past, but this time it's different," the antique dealer said. "A lot of money's involved. The piece wasn't mine, either. It was here on consignment."

"What are we talking about exactly?"

"A brown glazed earthenware pot about so high." The dealer held his hands a foot and a half apart. "It's called Mormon pottery and dates from about 1875. What makes this piece special is the signature. Eardley Bros, Seventh Ward."

"How much was it worth?" Traveler asked.

"The owner wants four thousand dollars. I was asking five. Not a bad price, really. I've had interest from the church museum."

"Was anybody else in the shop at the time?" Traveler asked.

"I was with a customer in the back, but I still had a good view of Bill and Charlie. I always try to keep an eye on them, since they insist on tithing me, as they call it."

"Did you actually see them take the pot?"

"I saw Bill slip something under his sandwich board. When I went to see what was missing, the Eardley was gone. I figured they thought it was just another piece of crockery.

But they denied taking it when the police caught up with them."

"What does the owner say?"

"She won't press charges if we get it back."

TWELVE

Bill refuses bail," Charlie Redwine said the moment Traveler came through the Chester Building's revolving door.

Behind Charlie, Barney Chester nodded as if he'd been expecting that development all along. Behind Chester stood Nephi Bates, his earphones hanging loosely around his neck.

"Our Sandwich Prophet intends to become a martyr," Chester said. "His word, martyr. He blames the church, of course, not his shoplifting."

Traveler grabbed the Indian by the arm. "Talk to me. What are you and Bill up to?"

Charlie pulled free of Traveler's grasp. "To us, the Era is our way of counting coup against the white man."

Traveler stared at the Indian, who usually answered with single words or grunts.

Charlie raised an eyebrow. "In my prophet's absence, I speak for him."

Bates's lips moved silently as if he were trying to memorize every word.

"Go ahead, Charlie," Chester said. "We've been waiting a long time to hear you speak for yourself."

The Indian unbuttoned the two top buttons of his check-ered shirt, reached inside, and pulled out his peyote bag. "I saw Bill in my dreams last night. You also, Traveler."

"And?" Chester prompted.

Charlie folded his arms, closed his eyes, and began nod-ding rhythmically.

"I understand," Chester said. "Charlie's a shaman in his own right. He intends to work magic to get Bill out of jail." Chester rolled his eyes at Bates. "I can't interpret more at the moment."

"You're starting to sound like Bill," Traveler said. "Run me upstairs, Nephi. I don't feel like walking."

Bates glared but headed for the elevator. Once inside it, he replaced his earphones and turned up the volume until "Jesus Wants Me for a Sunbeam" leaked out.

Traveler hummed along, carrying the tune all the way to his office, where his father was talking to Lael Woolley. She picked up the phone and began punching in numbers the moment Traveler sat opposite her in his own client's chair.

"She's calling the LDS mission in Germany," Martin ex-plained.

She started to smile, then broke it off to speak into the receiver. "This is Lael Woolley. I'm calling for a genealogy check on a German citizen, Karl Falke. We believe he lived in Munich before World War Two."

Since no one on the other end questioned her identity, Traveler assumed she'd taken care of that in advance. No doubt the present phone call was meant for show only.

"I'd like that report as soon as possible, and any other information you can get me on the Falke family. If you can't reach me at home, pass on whatever you get to Mr. Willis Tanner."

Out of Lael's field of vision, Martin raised an eyebrow.

She cradled the phone, leaned forward as far as the desk allowed, and peered into Traveler's eyes. "You see the kind of power you could tap into if you joined us."

With a grunt, Traveler slipped out of his client's chair and into his father's. "What Bill calls a posy pot turns out to be Mormon pottery. If we don't get it back, someone's going to have to come up with four thousand dollars."

"My uncle would probably consider that a sound investment for raising a fallen angel named Moroni," Lael said.

Martin sighed. "Bill told me it was a donation to his Church of the True Prophet. As such, he said he had every right to sell it."

Lael tugged at her bulky sweater until the fabric clung to her ripe breasts. " 'God ministered unto him by an holy angel, whose countenance was as lightning, and whose garments were pure and white above all other whiteness.' "

Traveler ignored the quotation. "Did Bill tell you who bought it?"

"One of the faithful, was all he would say."

" 'Depart from me, ye cursed, into everlasting fire, prepared for the devil and his angels.' " With that, she came around the desk toward Traveler. There wasn't room enough to get out of her way, so he stayed put. She bent over his chair and kissed him on the cheek. "I have faith in my Moroni."

She left the office while he was still wiping off her lipstick.

"Her calling the mission wasn't my idea," Martin said as soon as the door closed behind her. "She volunteered."

"I don't want her doing us favors," Traveler said.

"I'll pay it back if it comes to that."

"I don't think that's what she has in mind."

"Some women go for older men," Martin said.

"We're both older than she is."

"The Traveler Curse, that's what I call it. Handed down from father to son. 'He that looketh on a woman to lust after her, or if any shall commit adultery in their hearts, they shall not have the Spirit, but shall deny the faith and shall fear.' "

Traveler was about to dredge up a comeback from Sunday school when the phone rang.

"Mo," Willis Tanner said immediately, "our German mission just called to confirm Lael's request. Have you taken her on as an assistant?"

"Get to the point, Willis."

"I gave them the go-ahead, if that's what you mean. Even as we speak, missionaries are being dispatched to do your dirty work."

"I didn't ask her to make the call," Traveler said.

"I hope you know what you're doing, Mo, fooling around with the prophet's grandniece."

"You know better than that."

"Do I?"

"You sound like you're up to something, Willis."

" 'My Lael needs protection,' the prophet told me."

"Not from me," Traveler said.

" 'I won't be here forever,' the prophet said. 'Who will watch over her when I'm gone?' "

"That's one job I don't want, Willis."

"That's what I hoped you'd say."

THIRTEEN

The sun was setting when Traveler parked in front of the police building on Fifth South. He got past the metal detector only to be caught by Sergeant Aldon Rasmussen.

"I should have been off duty half an hour ago," the sergeant complained.

"That sounds like you've been waiting for me."

Rasmussen was a tall, gangly man, whose goal in life was to prepare for retirement. To that end, he'd been selling real estate on the side for years, using his wife's license to shield him from charges of moonlighting. He was also a part-time dealer in sports memorabilia, though he claimed the enterprise was only a hobby.

"I have a message for you," Rasmussen said. "I even copied it down."

He handed Traveler a piece of scratch paper on which was written, " 'Beware of false prophets, who come to you in sheep's clothing, but inwardly they are ravening wolves.' "

"Willis Tanner?"

"Someone is watching over you, that's for sure." The policeman winked. "I suppose you want to see the sandwich man? I hear he's refusing bail."

"I hope to change his mind."

"Are you selling anything?" Rasmussen asked.

"You own most of my life already."

"How many local boys played linebacker in the pros?"

"You got the last of it when I gave you my shoulder pads."

"Football cards are starting to get hot. I have a few you could sign for me. Too bad you didn't play baseball. Some of those cards are worth a fortune these days."

"I'd like to see the arrest report, too."

"It's waiting on my desk," Rasmussen said. "All you've got to do is sign the cards."

Traveler's fingers were cramping by the time he got through a two-inch stack of football cards.

The arrest report confirmed what Davis, the antiques dealer, had said. Clipped to the report was a facsimile of a receipt from Era Antiques: *On consignment: one Eardley Bros/Seventh Ward earthenware jar, estimated value $4,000.*

"It doesn't make sense," Traveler said. "Bill doesn't know anything about Mormon collectibles. Neither does Charlie."

Rasmussen began sealing his signed football cards in individual plastic envelopes. "It's always nice when we can clear our books with a conviction."

"They've never taken anything worth more than a few dollars before. Usually they peddle it to me and I return it to the Era along with a penalty fee."

Rasmussen stood up to peer over the escrow walls on either side of his desk. When he sat down he said, "There are lots of people around here who'd like to see your friends in jail."

"So?"

"I have more cards at home," Rasmussen said.

"I'll sign them any time you want."

The sergeant pursed his lips for a moment. "Could be

somebody around here tried to get the man at Era Antiques to ID the Indian, too. Lucky for Charlie, the dealer stuck with the Sandwich Prophet."

"I might be able to come up with a jersey," Traveler said.

"I'll keep that in mind for the future. Right now, the only thing else you're getting from me is ten minutes with the sandwich man."

Bill wouldn't look Traveler in the eye.

"I've talked to the antiques dealer," Traveler told him. "A lot more than a few dollars is involved this time."

Bill continued to stare down at the lawyer/client table in front of him. His hands were out of sight, folded in his lap. His orange, jail-issued jumpsuit gave his skin a jaundiced tint.

Without looking up he said, "On behalf of the Church of the True Prophet, I thank you for past donations."

"You were seen taking the vase. The antiques man will have to testify against you if it comes to a trial."

"A prophet expects harassment." Bill's voice lacked its usual conviction.

"They're really after you this time, so don't expect probation."

"Jail is full of lost souls in need of saving."

"You'll find even more of them in state prison," Traveler said.

Bill twitched.

"Look at me," Traveler said.

Slowly, Bill raised his head. His cheek had swollen to the point where it distorted his entire face.

"Your tooth is worse, isn't it?"

"I need my disciple, my medicine man."

"If you're in pain," Traveler said, "they'll have to provide you with a dentist while you're here."

Bill raised a shaky hand to his face. "My cellmate warned me against it. Once they get you in the chair, he says, you're fair game. They tie you down and go to work. Under the drill, everyone confesses."

"You don't believe that."

Bill swallowed so hard his Adam's apple shimmied. "I'm afraid, Moroni."

"Stop playing martyr, then. I have your bail in my pocket."

The Sandwich Prophet took a deep breath, grimacing as air hit his bad tooth. "I have sinned, Moroni. Pride made me turn away Barney and your father when they came here offering to help."

"I can have you out of here in less than an hour."

Bill nodded.

"Before I go, I want to know why you stole that Mormon pottery."

"If you hurry, I've still got time to make my eight o'clock dinner with Lael." Bill sounded confident again.

"That was last night."

"It's her treat this time."

"Talk to me about the Mormon ware."

"It was a posy pot, nothing more."

"Where is it, then?"

"We're talking tithing here, Moroni. That comes under freedom of religion, which means you're messing with my constitutional rights."

"Why are you lying to me?"

Bill wiped his hands on the front of his jumpsuit. "Are you going to bail me out of here or not?"

Sighing, Traveler stood up. "I'll be waiting for you out front with the truck."

"Don't bother. I'm going to see a dentist before my date with Lael."

"Where will you find one at this hour?"

"That's the difference between us, Moroni. I have faith. I know God takes care of his lost children."

* * *

Traveler was waiting across the street when Bill left the police building. The Sandwich Prophet looked around carefully, a waste of effort at that time of night, before heading west on Fifth South. Since he was on foot, Traveler walked too.

At State Street, Bill turned north. The bright lights and empty sidewalks forced Traveler to fall back far enough to avoid being seen. When Bill crossed the street at Exchange Place, he started jogging west toward Main Street. By the time Traveler reached the corner, Bill was in full flight. He disappeared a block later where Exchange Place dead-ended into Main Street.

Traveler was out of breath when he reached Main. There was no sign of Bill. No stores were open in the immediate area. The Boston Building, on the north side of Exchange Place, showed only dim lobby lights. Its companion on the south side, the Newhouse Building, was dark except for exterior spots.

Traveler tried the doors to both buildings. The Newhouse was open. He had to use his penlight to read the directory inside. Only one dentist was listed, Franklin Guthrie, DDS, on the fourth floor.

FOURTEEN

At sunrise the next morning, Traveler was on his way to Kearns. When he was a boy, Kearns was considered a long drive out in the country. Now it was just another suburb, ten miles west of the temple in downtown Salt Lake.

Kearns began as an air force base in 1942. Before the war was over, a thousand buildings had been constructed, barracks, mess halls, chapels, warehouses, enough to make Kearns Utah's second-largest city.

The Nauvoo Techtronics plant included half a dozen leftover Quonsets along with a remodeled barracks and a new black glass cube. Grant Hansen, Otto Klebe's brother-in-law, was waiting in front of the cube. On the phone the night before, he'd insisted on a 6:30 A.M. interview.

Traveler swallowed a yawn and shook hands.

"Sorry about the hour," Hansen said, "but Mr. Klebe insists that his managers set the example, first man in, last man out. You know how the Germans are."

Behind Hansen, a uniformed guard unlocked the door to the cube. The sound of it made Hansen sigh. "I could have retired two years ago at sixty-five."

Traveler nodded sympathetically. Hansen, with his sagging body, white hair, and pale, translucent skin, looked seventy-five. He was wearing a winter overcoat against the chill wind blowing off the Wasatch Mountains. Yesterday's mild spring weather had given way to heavy cloud cover and the smell of rain, snow if the temperature dropped another ten degrees.

"This is Mr. Traveler," Hansen told the guard. "He'll need a visitor's pass."

Once the guard had clipped a plastic badge to the lapel of Traveler's tweed jacket, Hansen led the way to a nearby office. The sign on the door said EMPLOYEE INTERVIEWS. The room, ten by ten with a single Formica-topped table and two plastic chairs, was as bleak as the one where Traveler had interviewed Bill at the police building.

"You'll have to be out of here by eight," Hansen said as soon as they were seated in facing chairs. "Mr. Klebe is due in from Brigham City at eight-thirty to inspect the plant." He didn't sound happy about the prospect.

"Is that normal procedure?"

"He called late last night, though I don't see why that's of interest to you."

"As I told you on the phone," Traveler said, "I was in Brigham City yesterday when Mr. Klebe gave me your name."

Hansen's eyes narrowed momentarily. "Are you working for him?"

Traveler shook his head. "I'm trying to locate a former German prisoner of war. Your brother-in-law said you might remember a man named Karl Falke."

"Knowing my brother-in-law, he probably forgot to tell you that I was a captain in the U.S. Army. I was in charge of a POW camp. I had a platoon of guards and several hundred prisoners under my command. Now everything's upside down. The Germans and Japanese own everything. Look at my brother-in-law. You know why he's here in this country, don't you?"

Hansen jabbed himself in the chest with his thumb. "Because I sponsored him. I helped him emigrate here. I put myself on the hook for him financially and promised the government he'd have a job."

He glared at Traveler expecting a response.

"I hope he appreciates what you did for him," Traveler obliged.

"My father was a car salesman. A good one, too. The war almost did him in, though, because there wasn't much stock to sell in those days. When he finally managed to swing his own dealership, the war was over. Maybe you remember Hansen's Kaiser-Frazer. Our showroom was down on south State Street. You know what happened to those cars, of course. They were ahead of their time. That's why General Motors and Ford forced them out of business. It ruined my father. Me, too, for that matter. Not my brother-in-law, though. He came out smelling like a rose. How he did it, I don't know. He came to this country without a penny to his name. The next thing you know, he's investing in property. That's how I came to be working for the enemy. What do you think about that?"

Traveler hesitated, figuring any answer would probably be the wrong one.

"The prisoners' lives were in my hands," Hansen went on suddenly. "That goes for Otto, too. He was in my convoy, the one I headed up when we transferred POWs down south to Cowdery Junction to help bring in the sugar beets. That's where he met my sister, Norma, the times when she used to come down south to visit me. The situation was quite informal, you understand, with prisoners out in the fields working like regular laborers."

"Do you remember any of the prisoners' names?" Traveler asked. "Or even the guards'. Anything would be helpful."

"The men under my command weren't exactly one-A. In any case, the only German I remember is the one I'd like to forget. One name sticks, though, a guard named Maw, like old Governor Maw, only they weren't related. My Maw was an old guy back then, recycled from World War One. He was a local, though, from right there in Cowdery Junction. That was the only reason we took him on, so we'd have someone who knew the area. He must be dead by now."

"I understand there were deaths in Cowdery Junction," Traveler said.

"I was gone by then, thank God, back to Camp Tremonton."

"I'm surprised you don't remember Falke's name. He was the only escaped prisoner never accounted for."

"That I remember, but not the name. I made it a policy not to fraternize. My sister should have followed my example."

Traveler pushed back his chair and stood up.

"She's the one you should talk to, you know. The war changed her life more than it did mine."

"Your brother-in-law didn't give me the chance yesterday."

"She'd like to get a few things off her chest. That's why she came down from Brigham City with Otto, expressly to see you. She's at my house right now. Otto insists on staying with us when he's in town. He says it's to save on hotel bills, but I know he likes to keep an eye on me. He treats my wife, Juanita, like a maid. That's why she's staying with her sister out in Bingham Canyon."

Hansen led the way back to Techtronics's main entrance. "I shouldn't be telling you any of this. But what the hell. My retirement's already vested."

The guard took back Traveler's visitor's pass.

"My address is 42 Rigdon Avenue in Bacchus," Hansen said when they reached Traveler's truck. "Keep an eye out for my brother-in-law's Mercedes. I don't want you walking in on Norma until he's left for the plant."

FIFTEEN

North from Kearns, State Highway 111 ran along the base of the Oquirrh Mountains to Bacchus. Originally a small company town created by Hercules Powder, Bacchus was on its way to becoming another Salt Lake suburb. The house on Rigdon Avenue dated from the turn of the century, one of those cube-shaped houses known as the Prairie School of architecture, though with typical Utah modifications: Corinthian columns holding up a Romanesque architrave posing as a porch roof. The entire structure set on a badly cracked concrete foundation, attesting to Hercules's explosive past.

Norma Klebe, wearing a white apron and knitted shawl over a flowered blue housedress, hunched her shoulders when she opened the door. She squinted at Traveler's face, then shifted from side to side to peer around him.

"Otto sometimes doubles back," she said, stepping out onto the porch to look up and down Rigdon. "It's a good thing you didn't park in front, Mr. Traveler. Don't just stand there, come in."

She closed the door and threw the deadbolt before escorting him into a small parlor whose walls were covered with faded paper depicting flowers similar to those on her dress. She drew the drapes, then shook her head and jerked them open again. "This time of the morning a closed house might look suspicious."

"Why don't you call Techtronics," he said, "and make sure your husband's arrived."

"What a good idea." She tucked a stray hair into the bun at the back of her head. "I'll be right back."

After she left the room, he could hear her talking on the phone, though without being able to distinguish the words. After her voice faded, water began running somewhere deep in the house.

He looked around for a place to sit. The room held one fragile-looking Victorian sofa and four chairs, all upholstered in ornate needlepoint. Crocheted antimacassars were pinned to every arm and headrest. None of the furniture looked capable of holding his 220 pounds.

"We'd better move into the TV room," she said when she returned. "These are all family heirlooms my brother inherited from our parents. I wasn't so lucky. Otto didn't bring anything with him from Germany."

The TV room, furnished with a Naugahyde sofa and two Barcaloungers, had originally been a back bedroom. All three pieces of furniture faced a large-screen television set; all three had knitted afghans folded over their backs.

"Don't worry, Mr. Traveler. My brother has promised to call the moment Otto leaves the plant, so we don't have to keep an eye on the street. Even speeding he couldn't get here in less than five minutes. It's a ten-minute drive normally. That's why my brother lives here, because Otto insists that his managers be within ten minutes of their work."

She pointed to one of the loungers and waited for him to settle in before perching on the edge of the sofa.

"There are times when I wanted to hire a detective myself," she said. "The trouble is, when you go looking for something, you might not like what you find."

Traveler stared at her until she lowered her eyes. Finally, he took out a business card and handed it to her.

She tucked it away before continuing. "It's not Otto's fault the way he is. He became an American too late in life. I should have realized that. Are you married?"

He shook his head.

"I said my vows in the temple. They say that seals me and Otto together for time and eternity. Do you believe it?"

Traveler knew better than to answer a question of theology.

Norma closed her eyes. "It seems a long time to pay for a mistake."

After a pause Traveler said, "Do you know anything about Karl Falke?"

Her eyes opened but looked unfocused. "The war years were the best I ever had. Before then, the best I could do was a part-time job. Do you know what they paid back then? Twenty-five cents an hour. Utah had thirty-six percent unemployment at the time. It was old Governor Herbert Maw who did something about it. He fought to get war plants built here. One of those was the Ogden Arsenal, where I got my job. The men were away at war, so they needed us women. They started us at seventy cents an hour, and we worked forty-eight hours a week. After the war was over, they fired us, saying it wasn't ladylike to work. After what we'd gone through, too, working on guns and tanks salvaged from the battlefields, cleaning off the blood, skin, and hair."

She took a folded piece of yellowing paper from the pocket of her apron. "I dug this out of one of my scrapbooks after I met you yesterday, Mr. Traveler. It's from the church's *Relief Society Magazine* dated 1944. Women had no business working, they said. We should stay home where we belong and have babies. Listen to this part. 'Have the eyes of some in this day been so full of greediness that mothers have put in jeopardy the very souls of their children?' "

Her breath leaked away in a sigh. "Otto never let me work after we were married. He kept me pregnant and said God wanted it that way."

"Has your husband ever mentioned a man named Falke?" Traveler asked gently.

"You think I'm a backslider, don't you? You think I've fallen away from my faith. But I don't care. It was wonderful back then, having my own job and my own money. Once, I got my picture in the *Tribune* standing on one of those salvaged tanks. 'One of Utah's Rosie the Riveters,' the captain said. I sent a copy to my fiancé in the Philippines, but I don't know if he ever got it. His name was Orin Hale. He was listed as missing in action not long after."

She sighed deeply. "I kept in touch with Orin's parents until they passed away, even after I was married to someone else. The Hales were never satisfied, you know, despite the War Department declaring their son officially dead. Maybe they should have hired a detective like you."

Carefully, Norma refolded the paper and returned it to her apron pocket. "Listen to me, going on like this. You'd think I never got the chance to talk to anyone."

Traveler started to nod agreement, then caught himself.

"I met my husband when my brother was an officer at the POW camp in Cowdery Junction. Like all of the prisoners, Otto was starved for feminine company, not that anything went on between us, not then. That wasn't allowed. We talked, that's all, more and more as his English got better. He was a very handsome man in those days."

She smiled. "We women weren't supposed to fraternize, of course, especially in the camp area. It went on just the same, more so in Cowdery because it was such a small town. It was nice there until the shooting in Salina. After that everything changed."

She left the sofa to retrieve a needlepoint hoop and yarn from on top of the television set. As soon as she was seated again, she took up her needle and went to work, keeping her head down as she spoke. "My mother taught me needlepoint and crocheting, though Otto won't have it at home. He says it clutters the house."

"My mother was a great one for doilies," Traveler said.

Norma nodded without looking up. "After that last harvest in Cowdery, Otto was never the same. Of course, everyone connected with the place had been ordered not to talk about what happened. It would hurt the war effort, we civilians were told, though I could never see why since the war in Europe was already over."

She paused to thread a second needle with a different color yarn. "When Otto came back to this country and started courting me, we went for a drive and ended up in Cowdery Junction. He said he wanted to see the countryside again. We parked near the old campsite and were petting hot and heavy when he told me the prisoners' side of the story. They thought the camp guards had murdered their comrades. Some of the hard-core Nazis were even planning revenge, he said, though they never got the chance."

She pricked her finger and sucked it for a moment. "You probably think I'm senile, but I haven't forgotten about the man you're looking for. I probably knew him to look at but not personally, not by name."

Traveler started to get up.

"There's more, young man. My husband got a letter from Germany, from a woman named Falke. It was a long time ago, but I remember it because of Otto's reaction. He was terribly angry. 'The war is over,' he said. 'People should forget about it.' "

"What was in the letter?" he asked.

"It was in German, so I only know what he told me. The woman was looking for her husband, who never came home after the war. She wrote to us because of a letter she'd gotten years before from her husband, saying that Otto was his closest friend in the Cowdery camp."

"That's not what your husband told me."

"Otto said the woman was wrong, that her husband must have meant someone else. That's why he threw the letter away without answering it. That fact is, I'm surprised my husband talked to you at all. Like I told you, he thinks those days are best forgotten."

■————————■

"The man I'm looking for went missing right after those six prisoners died in Cowdery Junction," Traveler said.

She looked up from her needlework. "I'm sorry. I don't know anything else."

"Is there anyone in Cowdery Junction I could talk to?"

"The camp's not there anymore. It was gone by the time we took our drive back in 1949."

She left the sofa to replace her needlepoint on top of the television set. "There was a park where it had stood. There were even picnic tables. I remember thinking at the time that there should have been a monument of some kind. Instead, I got the feeling that someone had tried to erase all memory of what had taken place there."

"I'd like to speak with your husband again." Traveler got to his feet. "Do you know his schedule after he leaves the plant?"

"If I were a detective, I'd catch him at the Alta Club at one o'clock. He's meeting his lawyer and a couple of investors."

Norma's broad smile made Traveler wish he'd known her as a young woman.

"Thank you, Mrs. Klebe."

"I'd get there early if I were you. Otto has that German compulsion. 'Punctuality is next to Godliness,' he likes to say. That means he'll be there with fifteen minutes to spare."

Traveler had gotten as far as the door when she said, "I wouldn't have married him, you know. Not if my Orin had come back from the Philippines."

SIXTEEN

Lunchtime at the Alta Club was still two hours away when Traveler left Bacchus and headed for Salt Lake. From where he was, the west bench of the Oquirrh Mountains, he could see the Wasatch Mountains to the east. Brigham Young's wagon train had crossed those ten-thousand-foot peaks in 1847 to escape the Illinois Masons and politicians who'd murdered the first Mormon prophet, Joseph Smith.

Once hunkered down behind the Wasatch, Brigham Young laid out his City of Zion according to God's master plan, with the temple at the center. He decreed that every aspect of Mormon life would radiate out from that hub, a holy progression all the way to the city limits. These days, however, Brigham's vision ended at those boundaries, where the secular chaos of the postwar building boom had taken over. Greater Salt Lake, it was called now, with over a million people and everything that went with them.

By the time Traveler reached the temple intersection at the head of Main Street, hail was falling. For a moment, he was tempted to circle the block and take shelter in the Chester

Building. But the *Tribune* was only a block and a half away. If the newspaper's computers were on-line, he had more than enough time to research the official version of what happened in Cowdery Junction.

He ended up parking two blocks away and making a run for it. He was soaked by the time he reached the Tribune Building. The newspaper—originally founded by excommunicated Mormons to battle the church-owned *Deseret News*—had lost some of its teeth over the years but could still bite when provoked. The man with the sharpest incisors was Cody Peterson, a political reporter who'd gone to high school with Traveler and Willis Tanner. Peterson was a short, round man who indulged in Brooks Brothers suits because he claimed they were the best at hiding his pear-shaped body. He smelled of tobacco though he didn't smoke, a condition he achieved by filling his coat pockets with loose cigars. It was his way of thumbing his nose at the church's Word of Wisdom without endangering his health.

At Traveler's approach, Peterson pulled off his glasses and cleared his desk to arm-wrestle, a ritual he insisted on. He rolled up his right sleeve as far as it would go without removing his coat, then called over a couple of female colleagues to witness the spectacle. Both women looked young enough to be students.

"He wasn't trying," one of them said as soon as Traveler lost.

"It's fixed," the other added.

"It's a matter of leverage and muscle length," Peterson told them. "Pound for pound short guys have more power." He leered. "In everything."

"I suppose that's what you call male bonding," the first one said.

Both women walked away without looking back.

Peterson shook his head. "Pretty soon there won't be any men left in this business. Tell me what you want before affirmative action gets me thrown out on my ass."

"German prisoners," Traveler said. "Specifically those

held in Salina and Cowdery Junction during World War Two. One of them disappeared and I've been hired to find him."

Peterson whistled. "If you come up with the guy, I want him for my column."

"Six prisoners died just before my man disappeared. Their deaths may have been hushed up."

Peterson led the way to a computer terminal that accessed back issues. He attacked the keys as if he were pounding an old Royal typewriter. Salina popped up under the heading of *German Prisoners*. The machine-gunning there had made national news. The only mention of Cowdery Junction involved POWs volunteering to help with the sugar beet harvest. The headline read, GERMAN PRISONERS HAPPY TO HELP U.S. WAR EFFORT.

"The computer has only so much storage space," Peterson said. "When you get back that far, more than forty-five years, only the front pages of the first and second sections have been posted. We could go through back issues by hand if we have to, but it would be a bitch."

"You'd think six deaths would have made the front page," Traveler said.

Peterson tapped a computer key absentmindedly. "There was a war on, don't forget."

"It was over in Europe by the time he went missing."

"Still, six more dead Germans might not have made much fuss. Most likely they censored it like everything else during wartime. What do you say about the back issues? Do we schlep through them or not?"

"If I get desperate, I'll be back."

"Don't forget, Moroni. Either way, I expect to hear from you. My column has to be fed once a day."

Outside, the hail had turned to a cold, steady rain. A copy of the *Tribune* kept Traveler dry for a block and a half before disintegrating. After that, he took refuge in Sam Weller's bookstore, where Sam himself donated a plastic shopping bag as a makeshift umbrella.

Traveler was only mildly damp by the time he reached the Chester Building, where Mad Bill and Charlie were picketing out front. Bill's sandwich board, bleeding ink from every letter, read, END RELIGIOUS PERSECUTION. Charlie's hand-held picket sign said, END THE INDIAN WARS.

Rain had plastered their hair against their scalps. Bill's beard hung in strands like wilted dreadlocks.

Traveler herded the pair into the lobby where Barney Chester was waiting. It took the three of them—Traveler, Chester, and Charlie—to separate Bill and his soggy prophet's robe from the sandwich boards.

He spoke the moment he was free. "I won't be intimidated, Moroni."

"Bill's been to the dentist," Chester said. "He says you made him do it."

"I should have kept the pain," Bill added. "It was my way of being tested."

"He had his tooth out," Chester said.

"Did you finally go to Doc Ellsworth after all?" Traveler asked.

Bill folded his arms and pursed his lips. Charlie did the same.

Traveler shook his head and started for the elevator. When he saw Nephi Bates pointing at him with *The Book of Mormon,* Traveler veered into the stairwell. He was breathing heavily when he reached his office.

"I just got off the phone with Lael," Martin said as soon as Traveler opened the door.

Traveler sank into his own client's chair.

"She talked to that Breen woman on the Coast again," Martin added. "We've got another chance to find the boy."

"Where now?"

"Since Milford didn't work, Miz Breen now says she must have misunderstood Claire. She now thinks it was Milburn down in Sanpete County where the boy was adopted."

"That sounds like a maybe," Traveler said.

"Could be he's the only grandson I'm ever going to get."

"Do you believe Lael?"

"We can't afford not to," Martin said. "Besides, what would it hurt to check out Milburn?"

"I've got work to do in Cowdery Junction."

"Come over here." Martin tapped the glass on his desk that covered a Utah map. As soon as Traveler was looking over his shoulder, Martin ran a finger down the center of the state, following I-15 to Spanish Fork. There, his finger detoured onto Highway 89 until it reached Milburn. "It's practically on the way."

"Does that mean you're coming with me?" Traveler asked.

"I'd better, since you still have a few things to learn."

Traveler grunted. "I don't suppose you'd have a necktie handy?"

"I taught you better than that. A detective has to be ready for all occasions." Martin opened a desk drawer and removed a clip-on paisley. "Where are we going?"

Traveler retrieved a conventional striped tie from his own desk and began struggling with a Windsor knot. "We're lunching at the Alta Club."

Martin tucked his tie into place. "You must have missed part of my lesson. It's harder to strangle someone wearing a clip-on."

Traveler ran a finger around the inside of his collar. "Then it's a good thing I'm taking you along as protection."

SEVENTEEN

The Alta Club, originally founded as a Gentile men's club excluding Mormons, stood one block east of the temple and catercorner from Beehive House, once Brigham Young's official residence. The club's membership had been integrated years ago, though Mormons were still said to be in the minority.

Traveler and Martin got past the doorman by saying they were lunching with Otto Klebe. Inside, walnut paneling and gold-framed oil portraits glowed in soft light from converted gas chandeliers and wall sconces. Oriental carpets muffled their footfalls as they headed for a waiting room filled with hand-carved desks, wingbacked chairs, and love seats. Traveler and his father sank into side-by-side Chippendales where they could watch the foyer.

"They say the food here is superb," Martin said quietly.

"I don't think we'll get the chance to eat," Traveler whispered back.

"Your mother always wanted me to join a place like this.

Private clubs have bars, I used to tell her. That's one of the reasons they exist, to get around Utah's liquor laws. You know what she said to that?"

Traveler shook his head as was expected of him.

" 'Drinking wouldn't be a sin if you did it in a place like that.' Kary's words exactly. Your mother could accommodate just about anything if it suited her purpose. Do you remember when the colleges were recruiting you out of high school? Your mother and I weren't living together at the time, but she came to me all excited when Notre Dame showed interest. She'd seen that Knute Rockne movie. I told her you couldn't play there unless you joined the Catholic Church. What do you think she said to that?"

Traveler resisted the temptation to answer.

"She got that shrewd look of hers, you know the one, and said, 'A little religious instruction would be good for my Moroni.' 'He'd have to go to chapel every day,' I told her. 'It does a man good to get down on his knees,' she answered."

Martin rubbed the knees of his corduroy trousers and grinned. "Do you know what she said when nothing came of Notre Dame?"

Before Traveler could respond, Otto Klebe entered the vestibule and began shedding his trench coat. Underneath, he wore a dark blue three-piece suit.

Traveler and Martin, walking side by side, moved to block his way.

"What are you doing here?" he demanded.

"There are some things we have to talk about," Traveler said.

"I'm meeting someone for lunch."

"We haven't eaten yet," Martin said.

"Don't be ridiculous."

"It's best to keep your voice down in the Alta Club," Martin said. "God knows what they'd do if we made a ruckus and started yelling."

Klebe clenched his teeth.

Martin continued. "The way I hear it, most of the members here are old-time families. They don't take in newcomers like yourself."

"I could buy and sell most of them."

"You're not a member, then?"

"I'll give you ten minutes. We can talk in the bar."

To get served, Klebe had to admit to the bartender that he was there as a guest of his lawyer. Traveler recognized the attorney's name, a senior partner in a third-generation Gentile firm.

"He's putting me up for membership when the time's right," Klebe said when their drinks had arrived. "Lucky for you two they still blackball here. Otherwise, I'd have thrown you out myself."

He ran a hand down the front of his vest and adjusted a gold watch-chain. "Looking at me, you wouldn't know I started out life in Utah behind barbed wire, living in a tarpaper barracks with a coal-burning stove for heat. Then and there, I promised myself I would not only survive but prevail. For years I've been buying up the land around Cowdery Junction. And a hell of a lot of Salina to boot. It's fitting, don't you think? A German owning the land where his fellow prisoners were murdered."

Klebe forced a smile. "When the war ended, the people in Cowdery Junction were among the casualties and didn't know it. Hawaiian cane made them as redundant as their sugar beets."

"You lied to us," Martin said, raising his voice slightly. "We want to know why."

Klebe, looking anxious, glanced at the bartender.

"Karl Falke," Martin continued at higher volume. "You told us you didn't know him well."

Traveler spoke more softly. "We've learned he was your closest friend in camp."

"Who told you that? My brother-in-law, I suppose."

"Is it true?"

Klebe spoke quietly, submissively. "I didn't want to tell

you about it, because I was embarrassed. You see, Karl Falke helped me once when I didn't have the guts to stand up for myself. He took my side against some hothead Nazis who claimed I was fraternizing with the enemy because of Norma. I didn't reciprocate, though, when they got on his case."

"But you were friends?" Traveler said.

"Not for long. There were rumors that traitors would be killed when we returned to Germany. That's when Falke told me about his plan to escape."

"Tell us about it," Traveler said.

"There was no place to go but the desert, so I told him no, I wouldn't join him."

"Is that when he disappeared?"

Klebe nodded.

"Did you ever hear from him again?" Martin asked.

"Never. I figured he probably died in that desert. That, or he's living somewhere under an assumed name."

Klebe had offered to arrange lunch for Traveler and his father at the Alta Club, but Martin had his mind set on Branning's Chili Parlor, a long narrow cafe halfway between First and Second South on State Street.

He and Traveler were sitting down to Morrison meat pies smothered in chili when a tall man, whose bearing was so upright he looked like he was wearing a back brace, came in and sat beside them. The newcomer had on tan cuffless slacks and a matching sports jacket. His brown shoes were spit-shined. Traveler would have recognized him even without his military haircut. "Colonel Stiles?"

The man nodded.

"You look much like your father. This is my father, the founding half of Moroni Traveler and Son."

Stiles stared skeptically at Martin.

"Some genes are stronger than others," Martin said.

"How did you find us?" Traveler asked.

"I went to your office. A man named Chester told me Thursday was your day for Branning's chili. I know how you feel. I come here every time I'm in Salt Lake on leave."

He signaled, almost a salute, for a bowl of chili. "Before I forget, Chester sent you a message. Someone named Lael has vital information for you and will be waiting at the office."

When Stiles's chili arrived, he added Branning's special TNT sauce, took a quick mouthful, and let out a long sigh of contentment.

"Are you on leave now?" Traveler asked.

He shook his head while continuing to chew. "I came home to take care of my father's affairs."

"Your father told me you were assigned to the Pentagon."

"On track for a star, or so they say. The trouble is, it won't be in time for my father to see it. His dream is to have a general in the family."

"And yours?"

"At the moment my main concern is the twenty-five hundred dollars my father paid you."

"I tried to talk him out of it," Traveler said.

"So he told me."

"All your father has to do is say the word," Traveler said. "We'll refund his money."

"Less expenses," Martin added.

Stiles concentrated on his chili for a while. So did Traveler and his father.

Finally the colonel pushed his plate away. "You've had three days on the case. Is there anything I can report to my father?"

"It's only been two full days," Martin corrected. "In any case, we report only to our clients directly."

"I have his power of attorney."

"If you'll follow us back to the office," Traveler said, "we'll work out our expenses and refund whatever's left over."

———————

"Forget it," the colonel said. "I want my father's last days made as easy as possible. Settling the past is important to him. Having someone like yourself try to set matters right will be good enough, he says, even if you fail. Now that I've met you two, I don't think his money's being wasted."

Traveler stared at his father, who said, "We might as well tell him what we've done so far."

Traveler nodded. "We've spoken to a number of people who were involved with the POW camps. Tomorrow we plan a visit to Cowdery Junction. That means paying for a motel, mileage, and other on-the-road expenses."

"My father found a letter that might be of help," Stiles said. "It's from the missing man's wife. It's a translation, of course, which my father had done at the time. That was back in July 1949."

Dear Major Stiles,

As you know, I have written to your government in Washington, also to the President, Mr. Truman, about the fate of my husband, but only you were kind enough to answer a poor widow. I call myself that because I feel certain in my heart that my Karl would have returned to me if he were still alive. Though what he would think of me I don't know. I have become an old woman before my time.

I know you've tried to find Karl for me without success. Perhaps you could locate his friend. Unfortunately, I don't know the man's name for sure, only that Karl had one close friend in camp. He was never named in Karl's letter because of wartime censorship, but I believe they had met before, during training when my husband was first called into the army. If that is so, I met him when Karl brought him home on leave. His name was Otto Klebe. I have tried to locate him here in Germany, but was told that he immigrated to America. Maybe you could help me locate him.

Yours sincerely,
Frieda Falke

After Traveler read the letter, he gave it to his father.

"Is censoring names normal procedure?" Martin asked once he'd read it.

"Absolutely," Stiles said. "Anything that might possibly be used as a code is deleted. Musical notes, quotations, shorthand, just about anything."

"Did your father look for this Klebe?"

"Now's not the time to ask him, I'm afraid. He's just been hospitalized. The doctors say the end is very close, only a matter of days. I hope to God you can put his mind at rest before it's too late."

EIGHTEEN

A tan four-door sedan, so generic-looking that it was obviously official, was parked in the loading zone in front of the Chester Building. There were two men inside, also generic. Less than a foot ahead of their vehicle, next to a fire hydrant, stood Lael Woolley's BMW.

Traveler squeezed into the yellow zone until his truck nudged the sedan's rear bumper.

"They'll never get out," Martin said.

"Church security ought to know better," Traveler answered.

For once the sidewalk in front of the Chester Building was clear. Traveler glanced across the street at the temple. There was no sign of Mad Bill or Charlie, unusual now that the weather had reverted to spring sunshine, with the last of the thunderheads about to disappear behind the eastern front of the Wasatch Mountains.

Traveler was heading for the brass revolving door when he spotted Bill and Charlie in the lobby, staring out at him with their noses pressed against the plate glass. For a moment,

Traveler thought they'd been scared off the sidewalk by Lael's watchdogs. Then he saw they were both wearing dark jackets over jeans, dress shirts, and ties.

Martin rapped a knuckle on the glass in front of Bill's nose. "I thought their dinner with Lael was last night."

Traveler followed his father through the door, which kept on revolving to admit the security men. Their appearance caused Bill and Charlie to retreat toward the cigar stand.

A hand fell on Traveler's shoulder. He spun out of reach.

The security men, in their mid-thirties and athletic-looking, shifted their feet as if expecting to be attacked. Both wore gray suits and nondescript ties. The shorter one, six feet as compared with Traveler's six-three, acted as spokesman. "We represent Mr. Willis Tanner. He wants you to know that he's been called to the Alta Club. He says you'll know why and prays that you'll take appropriate action to make certain it doesn't happen again."

"Tell Mr. Tanner I'm deaf to everything but person-to-person dialogue," Traveler said.

"Do you realize who Mr. Tanner is?"

"I should hope to hell we do," Martin snapped. "He grew up with my son here. Willis was a bad influence then and still is as far as I'm concerned."

The security men exchanged startled glances.

"That boy was a holy terror, let me tell you. He used to water my liquor so I wouldn't know he and Moroni were sneaking drinks. They weren't smart about it, though. Pretty soon there was nothing left but a clear liquid. That's when Willis got the idea of coloring it with food dye. I'd have caught on a lot sooner if I'd been much of a drinker. Instead, he taught my Moroni how to sin against Joe Smith's Word of Wisdom."

The pair fled.

Bill reappeared to say, "Lael's been waiting for you a long time, hours in fact."

Martin shrugged. "Let's go upstairs and get it over with."

"She's with Nephi Bates at the moment. He's teaching her the finer points of running an elevator."

Bates looked like a man in pain or ecstasy, it was impossible to tell which. The elevator's power had been switched off, allowing it to remain stationary while teacher and pupil worked the stop-start lever. Lael was straddling Bates's collapsible stool, causing her short skirt to ride high on her thighs. A snarling BYU cougar on her sweatshirt focused attention on the swell of her stomach and breasts. Charlie, his arms folded, was acting as passenger.

At Traveler's approach, she stood up, touched Bates on the shoulder, and said, "I'll tell Uncle Elton how kind you've been."

In an instant, his face changed; ecstasy wiped away all trace of pain. His lips moved but no sound emerged.

"You're right to pray for me," Lael told him. "My uncle will know that, too. Now, run us upstairs, will you? I have things to say to the Moroni Travelers."

"Martin," Traveler's father corrected as he stepped into the elevator. "That's the only name I answer to."

As Charlie started to exit, Traveler restrained him to ask, "Why the coat and tie?"

"We're paying homage," Bill answered. "By not changing our clothes, we're savoring the memory of last night's dinner with Lael as long as possible."

Traveler released the Indian. "You two stick around. We'll take you out to eat after we finish our business with Lael."

"Am I invited?" Lael asked as soon as the elevator started to rise.

"It's strictly stag," Martin told her.

Her pout triggered a sympathetic scowl from Bates.

"It's all right, Nephi," she reassured. "I was dining with the prophet anyway."

He looked awed all the way to the top of the Chester Building, where he fiddled with the stop-start lever until the elevator was aligned perfectly with the lip of the third floor.

"Don't forget your promise, Nephi," Lael said when he opened the grillwork gate.

He nodded and kept on nodding until he and his elevator dropped out of sight.

"What was that all about?" Martin asked.

Lael smiled. "He's going to keep an eye on you two for me."

"He already does that, if you believe Barney's theory that he spies for the church."

Smiling, Lael walked down the hall to their office, where she stood tapping her high heel impatiently until Traveler opened the door for her. Inside, she perched on the edge of his desk, exposing her taupe hose and slender legs to mid-thigh. He tried to avert his eyes, but not before she caught him staring. A look of triumph lit her face.

Martin got a good look, too, before collapsing into his own client's chair and closing his eyes.

Traveler moved behind his desk but didn't sit down. Instead he stared at the tabernacle dome across the street. "We got your message."

"Something about vital information," Martin added.

"Our mission in Germany sent a fax."

Traveler raised his eyes to the temple spire that held the golden image of the Angel Moroni. He wet his lips; he could still taste Branning's chili. He refocused on her reflection. "What did Germany have to say?"

She left her perch for his client's chair. "Karl Falke was born in 1920 and has been unaccounted for since 1945. His wife, Frieda, was born in Munich in 1922 and died in 1990. Forty-five years is a long time to be alone."

Traveler turned away from the window to face her. Her lips twitched, the flicker of a smile.

"They had one son," she said. "He died in the bombing when he was four. Falke's only sister, Elke, passed away in 1987. All her children were born after the war and know nothing about their missing uncle."

Martin's eyes opened. "That doesn't tell us anything we didn't know already."

"Cowdery Junction is still our best hope," Traveler said.

Lael tucked her hands inside the sleeves of her sweatshirt. "That's on the way to Milburn, isn't it?"

"If we take eighty-nine," Martin said, "it's no more than a couple of miles off the highway."

"The interstate's faster," Traveler said.

"We're talking about Moroni Traveler the Third," Lael said. "A son."

"Why should Milburn be any different from Milford?"

Lael's tongue ran along her upper lip. "I had a long talk with Stacie Breen. I reminded her that I paid a lot of money to find the boy. She said you'd have to know Claire to understand the problems involved. The confusion about Milford and Milburn, or maybe even Midway or Midvale, was Claire's way. She liked keeping you in the dark, Moroni, so you'd dance to her tune. At least, that's what Stacie told me."

With a sigh, Martin opened the middle drawer of his desk, extracted a notebook, and began thumbing through its pages. "Milburn, Milburn. Nope, there's no entry here. That's one cemetery I haven't visited yet."

NINETEEN

Traveler always thought of Duffy's rib joint as the Zang, a hangout of his youth. The Zang had been a combination beer bar and sandwich grill at the mouth of Edison Street where it ran into Third South. Duffy had changed the name and menu when he took over. His regime included a 5:00 to 6:00 P.M. happy hour and all the ribs a person could eat for five dollars. His profit margin, he once confessed to Traveler, was the vast amounts of beer necessary to cut the grease.

At the sight of Bill and Charlie, who jointly held the record for ribs consumed during a single sixty-minute period, Duffy limped out from behind the bar, shook his head, and groaned. "Bankruptcy, here I come." His limp, the result of trying to bounce one too many drunks, made him look as if he were dodging invisible obstacles.

"No ribs for us tonight," Traveler said to appease him.

"Make it four T-bones," Martin said. "We're celebrating. We'll have a pitcher of your best imported beer, too."

Duffy grinned at such a prospect and escorted them to a back booth. He even ignored Charlie, who immediately began carving Bill's initials into the already scarred tabletop.

"Anything to go with those T-bones?" Duffy asked.

Traveler raised an eyebrow.

"Yes, sir." Duffy saluted. "I'll bring your pot of tea right away." He limped away humming "Tea for Two."

"What are we celebrating?" Bill asked.

"We've got another lead on Moroni the third," Martin answered.

"We know. Milburn, Midway, and Midvale. Lael told us the story last night at dinner."

"We've only just learned about it."

Bill closed a hand over Charlie's Swiss Army knife. "I've come to know Lael's spiritual side. I'm certain she carefully chose the time and place to tell you. No doubt she waited for the moment when you'd be best prepared for such a revelation. As for me, my revelations come when I least expect them." His voice dropped to a murmur. "Sometimes when I don't want them."

"I'm making Lael a medicine bag," Charlie said.

"We've offered her honorary membership in the Church of the True Prophet," Bill added.

"What did she say to that?" Martin wanted to know.

Before Bill could answer, Duffy arrived carrying a tray. A large ornate English teapot and three matching cups were arranged around a pitcher of beer.

As always Duffy's tea came COD. Traveler slipped the man a twenty.

"Who's playing mother?" Duffy asked.

"I'll volunteer," Martin said.

Duffy arranged the cups in front of Traveler, Charlie, and Bill. "No cheating," Duffy said. "That tea's eighty proof. I want someone sober enough to drive."

As soon as Duffy retreated into the kitchen, Traveler poured three cups of whiskey. Martin poured the beer.

"Boilermakers," Charlie whispered, "often bring magical visions." He folded his knife and put it away.

"My word of wisdom exempts that which stimulates and enlightens," Bill said.

Traveler sipped. Bill and Charlie emptied their cups in a gulp, then needed half a glass of beer to cool their throats.

Martin replenished their whiskey and then raised his beer glass. "To enlightenment."

"To Lael," Bill amended.

By the time they'd toasted Lamanites (Indians and their ancestors, according to Mormon theology) and half a dozen of Brigham Young's fifty-five wives, Traveler figured Bill and Charlie were as maudlin as they were going to get.

"Don't you think it's about time you told me what happened at the antique store?" Traveler said.

"What we took," Bill said, speaking slowly and precisely to avoid slurring, "is nothing more than a crock pot."

"A piss pot," Charlie added.

"Where is it now?" Traveler asked.

Bill clasped Traveler's hand. "The Angel Moroni isn't the only contributor to the Church of the True Prophet."

Charlie snapped his teeth together. When no one responded, he snapped again.

"What are you trying to say?" Martin said.

The Indian removed the teapot's lid and peered inside the empty vessel.

"Well?" Martin glared at Bill. "You're his translator."

Bill folded his arms and leaned back against the booth's wooden wall.

Charlie upended the teapot while puffing out one cheek.

"I hear you," Martin said. "You're talking about Bill's tooth."

Charlie blew into the pot's curved spout, producing a melodious whistle.

"Charlie's right," Bill said. "It's best to tell your friends the truth. I traded the crockery for dental work."

"For God's sake. I already had Doc Ellsworth lined up," Traveler said.

"Charlie and I cannot accept personal charity. Everything supporters like yourself give us must be used for the Church of the True Prophet."

■—————————■

104

Martin snorted.

"I know I've sinned in the past," Bill said. "I've spent your donations on drink. But that was before I met Lael."

Charlie twitched.

Bill laid a reassuring hand on his disciple. "Not to worry. Wine is still one of my sacraments."

"Tell me the name of your dentist," Traveler said.

Bill manipulated his jaw and winced. "I'm sorry, Moroni. There's still crown work to be done. Until then, God's work must wait."

Charlie sucked on the spout.

Traveler and his father exchanged weary glances before ordering another service of eighty-proof tea.

TWENTY

It was nearly midnight by the time they left Duffy's. Martin drove, though Traveler was sober by then. From the Jeep's back seat, Bill and Charlie sang a pioneer hymn to the tune of "A Little More Cider." "Hurrah for the Camp of Israel! / Hurrah for the handcart scheme! / Hurrah! Hurrah! 'tis better far / Than the wagon and ox-team. / And Brigham's their executive, / He told us the design. / And the Saints are proudly marching on / Along the handcart line."

When they'd finished, Martin nudged Traveler. "Do you remember what I told you about your great-grandmother? She pulled a handcart all the way from Council Bluffs."

Since no reply was expected, Traveler merely grunted in the dark.

"When she got here, she raised hell because my grandfather was getting ready to take a second wife. 'Brigham's orders,' he told her. Do you know what she did?"

"Took after him with a broom," Traveler answered by rote.

Martin nudged him again. "Be sure you remember these

stories. Pass them on to Moroni the third if I don't get the chance."

They were heading up Main Street. At First South, Martin turned left to West Temple, then circled the block so he'd be on the right side of the street to park in front of the Chester Building.

At that time of night, there were only two other cars parked on South Temple, Lael's BMW and her church security escort, both in the red zone in front of the temple across the street from the Chester Building.

"The lights are on inside," Martin said. "Barney's still up."

"He'll provide the nightcap we need," Bill said.

"Revelations are a swallow away," Charlie added.

" 'And the arm of the Lord shall be revealed,' " Bill said.

Lael, who was sitting behind the cigar stand with Chester, wrinkled her nose when Bill came around the counter to hug her.

"Have you been waiting up?" Bill asked.

"I wanted to see what you get up to when I'm not around," she said.

"You're all drunk," Chester complained.

Lael nodded dramatically. "You should have taken me with you."

"You sound like my wife," Martin told her.

She escaped Bill to say, "What was Mrs. Traveler like?"

"Kary?" Martin scratched his head. "How should we answer, Moroni?"

Traveler was thinking that over when Bill spoke. "We came here for a nightcap."

Chester shook his head. "I'll make coffee if you want, but that's all. You already smell like West Temple winos."

Bill straightened his shoulders. "Charles, we'll use your nondairy creamer."

The Indian pulled out his medicine bag and held it at the ready.

"I give up." Chester began filling paper cups with the jug

wine he kept under the counter. He stopped at five, bracing the gallon jug on his hip, and looked at Lael. "What about you, young lady? Have they corrupted you too?"

" 'Strong drinks are not for the belly, but for the washing of your bodies,' " she answered from *The Book of Mormon*.

Traveler stared at his father, whose answering nod was barely perceptible. They both recognized that particular piece of scripture as one of Kary's favorites. Only in her case, she'd used it to condemn Martin's excesses while condoning her own.

Lael picked up the sixth empty cup and held it out toward the jug. "There are times when the body must be cleansed inside and out."

"I'll be damned," Martin said. "Mrs. Traveler used to say the same thing."

Lael's willful smile, Traveler thought, was much like his mother's. A smile that persisted until she got her way.

"A toast," Bill said. "To Lael."

Charlie handed out the cups of wine.

"To women," Martin added.

Everyone took a sip, though Traveler had the feeling that Lael only pretended to swallow. She saw him looking at her and winked.

"To Bill's secret benefactor," Traveler said. "His dentist."

"Why secret?" Lael asked.

"Tell her, Bill."

"No you don't, Moroni. You don't catch me that easily. So I have another appointment tomorrow at nine. What's the big deal?"

Lael pursed her lips. "What are you men up to?"

"I think it's time you went home," Bill said. His pleading eyes locked on Traveler's face.

Traveler said, "Come on, Lael. I'll walk you to your car."

Martin took her by one arm, Traveler the other. Together they led her across the lobby and through the revolving door.

"Do you think I need chaperoning?" With a toss of her

head, she indicated the church security men parked across the street. "I used to think it was my uncle who was having me followed, but it's Willis who's responsible. He says it's for my own good."

"He speaks for the prophet," Martin reminded her.

"With men you never can tell."

Martin sighed. "You would have got on with Mrs. Traveler. You speak the same language."

The three of them crossed South Temple Street in midblock. The BMW's remote-controlled locking system beeped at their approach.

Traveler opened the door for her.

Smiling, she eased into the BMW's bucket seat. "What did Claire look like?"

"A lot like Mrs. Traveler," Martin said.

"Do you have a picture of her?"

"Kary always said cameras didn't like her."

"What about Claire?"

Traveler closed the door on Lael, who immediately lowered the window.

"When you get to be my age," Martin said, "you can't remember what anybody looks like."

Traveler heard singing and turned around in time to see Bill and Charlie spill through the revolving door and out onto the sidewalk in front of the Chester Building. Charlie had the wine jug slung over his shoulder.

"Why are they the only ones who love me?" Lael asked.

"I met Kary when I was about your age," Martin said. "Moroni was old enough to know better when Claire came along."

"I'm talking about *me,*" Lael said.

"Now that I think about it," Martin said, "you do look like her a little."

"Which one?"

"Does it matter?"

"Damn you both." She revved the engine violently, then

U-turned and took off toward Brigham Young's statue at the head of Main Street with the church security chase-car in pursuit.

Martin waved a hand in front of his face to dispel the smell of burning rubber. "We Travelers always did have trouble communicating with women."

Shaking his head, Traveler took his father's arm and started back across South Temple.

"Look out!" Bill shouted.

Traveler heard an engine roar. He and his father both looked east, the way Lael had gone.

Instinct, abetted by peripheral vision, told him he'd made a fatal mistake. He snapped his head around as Charlie, pivoting like a discus thrower, hurled the wine jug in the other direction.

Traveler followed its trajectory and saw the high beams bearing down on him. He shoved his father one way and tried to roll the other, though he knew it was too late.

Glass shattered as the jug smashed against the windshield.

The vehicle veered, missing Martin but catching Traveler with a front fender. Breath exploded from his lungs as the impact hurled him through the air. He somersaulted once before landing on his shoulder in the gutter.

He fought off pain long enough to see the vehicle, a pickup truck heading east. In that instant, the driver turned, peering back through a rear window partially obscured by a full gun rack.

Get up, Traveler told himself. Run. The bastard might stop and use one of his rifles to finish the job.

Traveler opened his mouth to shout a warning to Martin. His cry was lost in the tearing impact as the truck rammed head-on into Brigham Young.

■———————■

TWENTY-ONE

Brigham Young, solid bronze standing on a solid granite base, had been built to last. So had those who shared his monument, including the bearded mountain man facing west toward the Chester Building. He held a bronze rifle and was often mistaken for Jim Bridger. The truck driver, hurled headfirst through an already cracked windshield, had bent the rifle slightly during impalement.

Willis Tanner, who'd been called to the scene by police, looked as shaken as Traveler felt. Tanner's nervous squint had closed one eye. The other one was blinking continuously and having a hard time coping with the glare from the portable floodlights that ringed the crash site.

"Who is he, Moroni?" Tanner asked.

Martin answered, "Considering his condition we haven't gone through his pockets."

"You said he tried to kill you. That ought to rule out strangers."

Traveler stared at the fingers of his left hand and flexed them. They moved well enough despite their numbness.

They'd get worse, he knew, the longer he waited to relocate his shoulder. He'd asked the paramedics do the job, but they turned him down, fearing medical complications and lawsuits.

"Maybe it was an accident," Tanner said.

"Bullshit," Martin shot back. "The bastard was aiming at us."

Tanner's open eye fluttered at the swear words. "Considering the kind of people you deal with, it's a wonder you've lasted this long."

Behind Tanner, three men from the coroner's office took hold of the body.

"Easy does it," one of them said.

"Please, God," Tanner murmured. "Don't let the rifle break."

"On three," one of the men said.

Traveler clenched his teeth and looked away.

"One, two, three . . . shit."

"There's a gouge in the granite, too," Tanner said. "That's going to have to be repaired."

The coroner's men went through a second countdown. This time the rifle came free and intact, though glistening wetly.

"Use your influence," Traveler said. "See if there's any identification on the body."

Rubbing his unruly eye, Tanner hurried over to Anson Horne, a police lieutenant assigned to police-church liaison. They huddled for a moment before Horne said something to the coroner's men. One of them, wearing surgical gloves, began searching the dead man's pockets. He found a wallet and opened it to the celluloid windows so that Horne could get a close look.

The policeman made notes before following Tanner over to where Traveler was sitting on the curb. Traveler stood to meet them, triggering a fresh stab of pain in his shoulder.

"You should be in the hospital," his father said as he, too, rose from the curb in front of the temple.

■———————■

"I hear you want an ID on the dead man." Horne was a second-generation cop and a third-generation bishop, who considered criminals and Gentiles as the enemy.

"When a man tries to run you down," Martin said, "you want to know his name."

"He missed you, didn't he?"

"Charlie Redwine diverted him with a bottle."

"So where is he?"

Off somewhere sobering up, Traveler thought. "He went for coffee."

"And your Sandwich Prophet?"

"They're together," Traveler said.

Pointing a finger at Traveler, Horne said, "Knowing those two, I could have them arrested for drinking in public. Better yet, maybe I can get the sandwich man's bail revoked."

"The last time we met," Traveler said, "it was me you threatened to arrest."

"If I had my way, it would be against the law for a Gentile to be named for our angel."

"Lieutenant," Tanner said sharply, "I want your cooperation." His tone implied that he was doing his job, speaking for the prophet.

Horne glared at Traveler before complying. "The dead man's name is Mahlon Broadbent. Does that mean anything to you?"

Traveler shook his head and looked at his father.

"I knew a lady named Broadbent once," Martin said, "but that must have been thirty years ago."

"According to the driver's license," Horne continued, "he comes from the town of Cowdery Junction. That's down south."

"Sevier County," Tanner said.

"I don't think I've ever been to Cowdery Junction," Traveler said.

The policeman eyed Martin.

"You know me and cemeteries, Lieutenant. Cowdery Junction is one I haven't visited so far. Now, if you don't mind I'd like to take my son to the hospital to get his shoulder looked after."

"Stop fussing," Traveler said. "You and Willis can put it back in place."

"Not me." Tanner backed up a step. "I remember what it was like the first time you did it at East High."

"You make it sound painful," Horne said.

"It makes me cringe thinking about it," Tanner answered. Horne smiled. "I'd be glad to volunteer."

TWENTY-TWO

Traveler made the mistake of moving when he woke up the next morning. Pain erupted in his shoulder, rushed down his arms, and started his fingers throbbing. He clenched his teeth and swung his legs out of bed. The scabs cracked open on his knees where he'd shredded them on Main Street.

He groaned.

"I've got coffee and codeine," his father called from the front of the house. A moment later he appeared in the bedroom doorway. "One pill or two?"

Traveler held up three swollen fingers.

Martin left the coffee cup on the nightstand and fetched a glass of water before counting the pills into his son's outstretched palm.

"I think we should forget about Cowdery Junction for a day or two, Mo."

Traveler washed down the pills. "Major Stiles doesn't have the time."

"Maybe so, but I still don't like what's happening. A POW goes missing fifty years ago, we're hired to find him, and suddenly someone from Cowdery Junction shows up and tries to kill us."

"What do you suggest, that we tell Lieutenant Horne the truth?"

"If I thought he'd believe us, yes."

Traveler stood up and winced.

"What's the hurry? Wait for the codeine to kick in."

"There's something I have to take care of before we leave town. You fix breakfast, I'll limber up in the shower."

"You ought to see a doctor."

"Would you settle for a dentist?" Traveler said.

An hour later, at 9:00 A.M. exactly, Traveler parked the Jeep in the loading zone in front of the Newhouse Building. The ten-story structure had been erected in 1910 to look like the commercial buildings in New York City, a failed attempt to turn Salt Lake's Exchange Place into the Wall Street of the West.

"You wait for me," Traveler said. "I'll see Bill's secret benefactor alone."

"You're in no condition to challenge anyone," Martin protested.

"He won't know that."

The smell of dental antiseptic greeted Traveler the moment he stepped off the elevator on the fourth floor. FRANK-LIN GUTHRIE, D.D.S.—black letters on a frosted glass door that looked as if it had been there since the Newhouse was built—was at the end of a long, linoleumed hallway.

The waiting room was empty, its chairs arranged facing a sliding glass window cut into the wall next to a door marked *PRIVATE*. A placard taped to the glass read, PLEASE HAVE A SEAT AND WAIT FOR THE NURSE.

Traveler went through the door without knocking. There was no nurse, only Bill laid out in the dental chair, the saliva ejector making sucking noises as it trailed from his mouth, and a short, burly dentist who looked strong enough to pull teeth with his bare hands.

Bill gagged and mumbled something that could have been "Moroni."

Startled, the dentist turned away from his patient to face Traveler, the drill in his hand aimed like a weapon.

Bill pulled the saliva ejector from his mouth. "Please, Moroni. Not now."

The dentist looked from Traveler to Bill and back again as if gauging his chances if it came to a fight. Then, slowly, he deposited the drill in its holder.

Traveler sighed. Despite the pain in his shoulder, he felt like punching someone.

"You'd better give him the crockery," Bill said.

Guthrie shook his head. "You touch me and I'll sue."

"When Moroni gets that look," Bill said, "watch out."

"Aren't you forgetting something?" Guthrie said. "We're in the middle of a root-canal. If I don't finish before the novocaine wears off, you'll be screaming your head off."

Traveler smiled. "You're going to finish, all right. As soon as I get what I came for."

"I've got a lot of money invested."

"Did I ever tell you that Moroni played linebacker for L.A.?" Bill said. "Once he crippled a guy he hit him so hard."

Guthrie collapsed onto his dental stool; his shoulders slumped. "That urn was to be the centerpiece of my collection."

"Where is it?" Traveler asked.

He stared at a metal dental cabinet that took up most of one wall. "The bottom shelf."

As soon as Traveler had recovered the pottery, he asked Bill, "Why did you do it?"

"I wanted to be independent for once. I wanted to pay my own way."

"Why him?" Traveler glared at the dentist.

"He saw us once, Charlie and me, tithing at Era Antiques.

I wouldn't have taken it if I'd known how much the damned thing was worth."

"Next time you want independence," Traveler said, "get a job."

"I do God's work, Moroni. You know that."

TWENTY-THREE

After delivering the stolen Mormon pottery to Era Antiques, Traveler and Martin followed U.S. 89 down the center of the state, through Utah and Sanpete counties to Sevier County. Along the way, ramshackle barns and faded billboards advertising long-gone products—Mail Pouch tobacco, Nehi soda, Studebaker cars—gave Traveler the feeling he was ten years old again.

"I miss the Sunday drives we used to take when I was a boy," he said.

"The ones with or without your mother?"

A Dairy Queen went by, the only sign of fast food they'd seen for fifty miles.

"Nothing changes around here," Martin said. "It makes you realize just how good the old days were."

When Traveler reached the Milburn turnoff halfway down the state, he pulled the station wagon onto the gravel shoulder but kept the engine running. His shoulder ached from holding onto the steering wheel.

"What about it, Dad? Do you want to detour and go looking for Moroni the third?"

"As things stand, I'd better keep an eye on the one son I've got."

Traveler smiled.

"Don't get sentimental on me," Martin said.

Traveler opened the door and got out. "You drive for a while."

"Why didn't you say your shoulder was bothering you?"

As soon as they exchanged seats, Traveler fashioned a makeshift sling out of a dish towel he'd brought along and slipped his left arm inside. "We ought to make Salina by lunchtime."

Martin cruised Salina's two-block business district until he spotted the Salt Lick Broiler on Main Street across from the sheriff's office. He parked in front of the cafe, a narrow one-story building of rough oolite limestone, and then turned to his son. "It might be a good idea if we asked the sheriff where he eats."

Traveler untied the sling and winced. Immobility had caused his shoulder to stiffen.

Martin shook his head and started for the sheriff's office without waiting for his son's answer. Out front, two folding metal chairs stood on the sidewalk. A hand-printed sign behind the glass in the door said, HAVING LUNCH AT SALTY'S.

They recrossed Main Street and entered the cafe. There were no customers at the six-stool counter or at either of Salty's two tables.

"Today's special is a hot beef sandwich," the man behind the counter said. His faded bib apron and a straw cowboy hat looked as old as he did, somewhere in his fifties.

"We're looking for the sheriff," Martin said.

"The special goes off at one-thirty." The man nodded toward a grimy wall clock. "That gives you five minutes."

Martin looked at Traveler, who shrugged his agreement.

"Two specials," the counterman hollered through a slot cut in the wall behind him.

Traveler eased onto a stool. His father remained standing, which made their height just about equal.

The counterman removed his hat and ran a calloused hand over his gray hair. "Not many people come looking for the sheriff." His age, Traveler reassessed, was closer to sixty. A very fit sixty.

"It's not a criminal matter," Martin said. "Nothing to worry about."

"The sheriff's name is Wayne Woodruff," the counterman said.

"There was a prophet named Wilford Woodruff."

"There are several Woodruffs in these parts. Of course, there was a lot of polygamy around here in the old days." The man settled his hat on a plastic pie cover that was protecting a single slice of custard.

"Funny you should say that," Martin said. "I was just telling my son the old days sound pretty good to me."

The counterman winked knowingly. "If you believe rumors, they say there are still some closet polygamists around here. It gives a man ideas, doesn't it?"

"I've never had much luck with women," Martin said.

"Female-caused domestic problems take up most of the sheriff's time."

"The sign on his office says he's supposed to be eating here," Traveler said.

"He already did."

A hand slid two plates through the order slot behind the counter. The hot beef sandwiches—white bread topped by thin slices of meat and an ice cream scoop of mashed potatoes smothered in brown gravy—reminded Traveler of boyhood lunches at Woolworth's.

The counterman retrieved his hat from the pie cover. "Let me tell you about Salina while you're eating. We had to be settled twice, you know, once before and once after the Indian wars. Of course, the original families think of everyone else as outsiders."

Traveler took a bite and closed his eyes, seeing Woolworth's, Kress, and Grant's again, the magic places of his childhood.

"Smallpox started the war. The Ute Indians, who were dying like flies, decided to get even and started the Black Hawk War. Salina had to be evacuated for five years. Some say we never did grow very big after that. They also say our population is twenty-one hundred these days, but I'd say that was stretching it. The fact is, we've been going downhill since World War Two."

Martin snapped his fingers. "There was a scandal here in Salina, wasn't there? Something about German prisoners being machine-gunned in their sleep."

The counterman turned around and leaned his head into the order slot. "I'm taking off now, Salty. You'll have to do double duty."

When he faced Traveler and Martin again, he took off his apron, revealing a sheriff's badge and a holstered revolver.

"When city folk like you come asking questions, I start getting suspicious." He nodded at Traveler. "Especially when they're as big as you are."

Traveler removed his ID and placed it on the counter. Martin did the same.

The sheriff read them carefully. "That doesn't tell me why you're here or who you're looking for."

"It's a missing person," Traveler said.

"On second thought," the sheriff said, "let's not talk about it here. If we do, Salty will have it all over town. I'll be waiting in my office across the street when you're done with lunch."

"We can eat later."

The sheriff shook his head. "I insist." He left the cafe without another word.

Traveler and Martin spun around to watch him take down the Jeep's license plate number.

"This may be the sticks," Martin said, "but he knows enough to check us out before saying anything."

TWENTY-FOUR

By the time Traveler and Martin finished lunch, Sheriff Woodruff was sitting in the sunshine in front of his office, his cowboy hat over his eyes, his metal chair cocked against the drab oolite wall. The sign on the door still said, HAVING LUNCH AT SALTY'S.

At their approach, Woodruff settled his chair onto the sidewalk and got up to greet them. "As soon as I heard the name Traveler it clicked. There couldn't be two guys your size named for an angel. You played linebacker for L.A., didn't you?"

"Sometimes I feel like it was someone else entirely."

"The police in Salt Lake say I can trust you."

"Who'd you talk to?" Traveler said, thinking of his encounter with Anson Horne.

The sheriff adjusted his straw hat. "Before we go any further, I'd like to know why you're here."

Traveler and his father had already agreed on a straight-forward approach.

"A German prisoner of war," Traveler said. "A man

named Karl Falke went missing from the camp in Cowdery Junction in 1945."

"What's that got to do with my town? Cowdery's a dozen miles south."

"We've been told that a few POWs settled around here after the war. We'd like to talk to them if possible."

The sheriff opened his office door and turned the sign around. It now read, BACK IN AN HOUR.

"Salina may not be much to you Salt Lakers," he said, "but I've never had the urge to move on. Come on, let me show you around."

Woodruff's patrol car looked brand new. He drove it that way, too, a steady twenty miles an hour through the business district and the residential area, with Martin in the front seat and Traveler in the back. Woodruff slowed to a creep when he reached a dirt road leading to the town's rodeo arena, then rolled to a stop without raising any dust.

"This is where it happened," he said. "This is where they held the prisoners during the war. Every time I come here, I remember what it was like. I was just turning draft age when the war ended. Those buildings over there"—he pointed to a row of barrackslike wooden structures—"they were built back in the Depression by the Civilian Conservation Corps, but the army used them to house the soldiers who were guarding the prisoners."

Traveler tried to open the sedan's rear door but the handle wouldn't work.

"A missing person sounds safe enough," the sheriff said, eyeing Traveler in the rearview mirror. "But I'd still like to know how a man your size got himself hurt."

"Someone tried to run me down."

"The driver got killed trying," Martin added. "A man named Broadbent. Mahlon Broadbent from Cowdery Junction. Does the name mean anything to you?"

The sheriff shook his head too late; his eyes had already given him away. "There are a lot of Broadbents in Sevier

County. Now that you mention it, I think some of them did settle in Cowdery."

He stepped out of the patrol car and opened the rear door. "This place still gives me the willies," he said, heading for the corrals next to the grandstand area. "Because my father was sheriff here before me, I went with him that night."

Woodruff stopped in front of the corral and gripped the top rail. "The war was over, for Christ's sake. It shouldn't have happened. There was an ugly mood in town, a lot of talk about German atrocities. Even when my father told them a guard had gone crazy and shot the Germans in their sleep, a lot of people said they had it coming to them. Only they hadn't seen the blood and heard the screaming like me."

He paused to take a deep breath. "Things changed, thank God, when the wounded started coming into the hospital. My mother was a volunteer there, like so many of our neighbors. I remember her saying, 'They were just young men in pain. They could have been my son.' She was right, too. They weren't much older than I was. She kept asking my father, 'Why give the guards on those towers machine guns when the war was already won? There was nowhere for those men to go even if they tried to escape.' "

"That's one of the reasons we're here," Traveler said, "to find out why Karl Falke disappeared after Germany surrendered."

The sheriff took off his hat and wiped its sweatband with his fingers. "Escaped prisoners were handled by the army, not the sheriff, though my father was supposed to be notified."

"And was he?"

"He knew prisoners had escaped, but as far as I remember they were all recaptured."

"Does the name Falke mean anything at all to you?" Traveler asked.

The sheriff shook his head and started back to the car. He didn't say another word until he parked in front of the Salina

Hospital. "This is where we brought the wounded that night."

He motioned them out of the car. As soon as Traveler and his father were standing on the sidewalk, Woodruff said, "If you want to know anything else, you'll have to talk to Doc Sorenson. Keep one thing in mind, though. We're lucky to have a doctor in a town this size. So you be nice to Parley. Otherwise, you'll answer to me."

TWENTY-FIVE

The doctor's office stood across from the hospital in one of those bleak stone houses so common to rural Utah, a story and a half of oolite disguised as Victorian Eclectic.

There was no receptionist, only a bell for visitors to ring. The sound was still echoing when a tall, balding man with pale skin and blue eyes appeared in an open doorway. His white lab coat looked freshly starched.

"I'm Dr. Parley Sorenson." He shook hands before slipping on heavy, black-framed glasses to study Traveler's sling. "The sheriff didn't tell me you were hurt."

"It's on the mend," Traveler said.

Martin introduced himself and his son.

"I have an office in back." The doctor led them into a converted bedroom no more than ten by ten. The walls were painted an antiseptic white, though the original wallpaper's flower pattern was leaking through. A small sink surrounded by a plastic splashguard stood in one corner. An oak desk and matching bookcase filled with medical texts took half the floor space. Two patient's chairs were crowded into what

127

remained. Sorenson waited for them to be seated before moving behind the desk. "Sheriff Woodruff tells me you're looking into World War Two Salina."

"We're more concerned with Cowdery Junction," Traveler told him, "but we thought we'd start here."

The doctor sat back and laced his hands behind his neck. "There was a time when people thought Cowdery Junction might pass us by. Ever since the war, though, I'm sorry to say it's been shrinking away faster than we have. As for survivors of that time, there are plenty of them around town."

"A list of names would be very helpful," Traveler said.

The doctor shook his head firmly. "I see no reason to trouble people after all this time. I am willing to give some medical advice, though. That half-assed sling you're wearing isn't going to help your arm any."

Traveler flexed his fingers, which felt numb at the tips. "I rigged it myself."

"I hear that kind of thing all the time. Usually, it's after blood poisoning has set in."

The doctor left the room for a moment, but soon returned with an adjustable sling. "The sheriff told me you were looking for a missing German soldier."

"It's more complicated than that," Traveler said. "We're trying to clear the books for our client."

"An old man who needs help," Martin clarified.

"I'll need his name if I'm going to help you," Sorenson said.

Martin sighed and looked at his son. "Go ahead, Mo. You might as well tell him."

In detail, Traveler explained the situation, including the medical prognosis for Major Lewis Stiles.

When Traveler finished speaking, Dr. Sorenson took off his glasses and rubbed his diminished eyes. "You say he's already been hospitalized?"

Traveler nodded.

"I can call Salt Lake easily enough to verify that."

"We have no objection."

Sorenson took a long time polishing his glasses. Finally he replaced them and sighed. "My mother was the nurse on duty the day of the shooting. It changed her life. Mine, too, for that matter."

He walked over to stare at the framed degree on the wall. "She and Father saw to it that I went to medical school at the university in Salt Lake. When I graduated, I had offers to stay on at the U as staff, but coming home to practice was always my intention. I owed that to my parents."

"We'd like to meet them," Martin said.

"Mother's still a local practitioner and midwife when the occasion calls for it, not to mention my part-time nurse. She went out on a call not long before you arrived."

Traveler flexed his itching fingers.

"Do you mind if I have a look at your shoulder?" the doctor asked.

"Of course he doesn't," Martin answered.

Traveler clenched his teeth in anticipation.

"When did this happen?" the doctor said as he helped Traveler remove his shirt.

"There was an accident last night," Martin said. "I had to put my son's shoulder back into place with the help of a bystander."

Sorenson's fingers probed gently. "You haven't been completely honest with me." He began manipulating Traveler's arm. "The sheriff told me he called Salt Lake himself." The doctor increased the pressure. "He said you hurt your arm when Mahlon Broadbent got himself killed."

"He tried to run us down with a truck," Martin said. "All we did was get out of the way."

"Now comes the tricky part," Sorenson said.

He rotated Traveler's arm without warning. Something popped inside his shoulder. The sense of pressure began easing immediately.

Sorenson stepped back. "How does that feel?"

Traveler clenched his fist. "Better."

The doctor stepped to the sink to wash his hands. "The

Broadbents are one of our original pioneer families. The father, Owen, and his wife, Helen, God rest her, had four children, including Mahlon. His two brothers are good men, but my advice is to keep clear of them for a while."

"You mentioned your father earlier," Traveler said. "Was he connected with the hospital?"

"Only as a patient. He wouldn't be alive today if it weren't for my mother's nursing."

"He sounds like a man to talk to."

The doctor dried his hands and returned to his desk. "If anybody knows about the war days, it's my father. Usually, he won't talk about them, but he's agreed to see you and your father."

"How does he know we're here?"

Sorenson smiled. "When the sheriff called me, I called Ernie. God knows who he called. One thing you can count on, everyone will know you on sight before the day's over. By the way, my father asked me to invite you to dinner."

TWENTY-SIX

The smell of roast lamb was in the air as Traveler and his father got out of the car. Ernie Sorenson's house was a turn-of-the century bungalow with alfalfa fields on three sides. The veranda, running across the entire front, was cluttered with wicker rocking chairs, a glider-swing, and a nest of TV trays showing rings where sweating glasses had once stood.

Sorenson—gray-haired, sun-wrinkled, somewhere in his seventies—opened the screen door and stepped out on the porch to meet them.

"Welcome," he said, shaking hands and smiling. "The leg of lamb needs another fifteen minutes, so why don't we sit here for a while and enjoy the evening." He spoke with a faint accent.

"Are you German?" Martin asked.

"I never could get it out of my voice," Sorenson answered, taking the swing for himself, "much as I tried."

Traveler and Martin settled into rockers.

"Were you a prisoner of war?" Martin said.

"I thought you knew. I was one of the wounded when that guard started shooting."

Using his legs, he rocked the swing. "It was a stomach wound. They didn't give me much of a chance, but my nurse knew better. She's my wife now, Ruth Sorenson. I took her name when we married. Ernst Vogel died in that hospital, I told her, and was reborn as Ernie Sorenson. She's still nursing, too, out on a midwife call right now."

He sighed, smiling at his own memory. "After I left this country, I kept studying English and writing her. I kept it up until I was able to return in 1951. I'd have been back sooner, but we were sent to England for a couple of years to help rebuild what our planes had destroyed. By the time I returned, I was twenty-six and Ruth . . . well, she was an old maid by Utah standards. That's why we were in a hurry to have our son, Parley. He's named for one of the early Mormon apostles, you know."

He paused to stare at them. "I assume we're all Saints here."

Traveler shook his head.

"You wouldn't have a cigarette, then, would you?"

"Sorry."

"Ruth doesn't mind if I cadge one occasionally as long as I don't keep them in the house. Thinking about the old days makes me want a smoke. A soldier smokes every chance he gets. Take a break, take a smoke. Survive a battle and light up. The worst part of being captured was running out of smokes. That was 1944 in France for me, and the best thing that ever happened. Of course, I didn't realize until I went back to Germany in 1947 and saw the devastation. After that, Utah seemed like heaven."

He took a deep breath and expelled it out as if blowing smoke. "Look out there at the fields and the cottonwoods and the mountains. There's no place prettier. And this house. It's been in my wife's family for four generations. A man like me couldn't live this well in Germany."

Sorenson stared west toward the Fishlake Mountains.

"What I wouldn't give for some Utah Dust. That's what we called the Bull Durham we got in camp."

He leaned back, folded his arms, and closed his eyes.

"Where were you when the prisoners died in Cowdery Junction?" Traveler said.

"Still in the hospital, thank God. They told us we wouldn't be repatriated if we talked about it, though that was obviously a bluff, since none of us knew a damned thing. What I heard, I got secondhand from Ruth."

His eyes opened; he raised his head and sniffed the air. "I'd say we've got five more minutes before that roast starts to burn. Let's move into the kitchen."

They followed him through a small living room filled with pine furniture and handmade rag rugs, down a narrow hallway, and into a steamy kitchen where the heavy smell of lamb reminded Traveler of Sunday dinners from his boyhood. The Kelvinator stove was like his mother's; so was the Hoosier cabinet and pie safe built into the wall. Even the worn linoleum looked familiar.

Sorenson opened the oven door, adding to the room's heady aroma, and peeked inside. "All I've got to do is mash the potatoes."

Martin and Traveler volunteered to help, but Sorenson seated them in a breakfast nook, already set with paper napkins and silverware, and insisted on serving the meal himself.

After saying grace, he continued to speak between mouthfuls. "I remember my wife saying it was strange about those casualties from Cowdery Junction. They seemed to get better at first, then suddenly they were gone. Word around the hospital was that they'd been poisoned by someone who'd lost loved ones in the war."

He tilted his head to one side. "I knew the dead men by sight if nothing else. We'd been together in Cowdery Junction before I was loaned out to another farmer."

"Do you remember their names?" Traveler said.

Sorenson shook his head.

"What about Karl Falke?"

"Sorry."

Traveler held out the prisoner of war photo that had been taken when Falke was first processed at Fort Douglas.

"Yes. He was with me for a while. I always thought he was one of the six who died."

"Not according to Major Stiles," Traveler said.

"Him, I remember. He walked around like a ramrod. We all thought he'd have made a good Prussian."

"Can you tell us anything about Falke?" Martin asked.

"Not really. We weren't tentmates or anything like that. Like I said, I thought he was among the dead who'd been working at the old Broadbent farm."

TWENTY-SEVEN

It was dark by the time Traveler and his father drove away from the Sorenson house. Martin was behind the wheel, heading south on the Cowdery Junction turnoff, when flashing red lights appeared behind them.

Traveler twisted around in the passenger's seat, prompting a twinge from his shoulder. "He's got his high beams on, but I think it's the sheriff."

Martin pulled onto the gravel shoulder and left the motor running. Traveler opened the glove box but didn't take out the .45.

The cruiser parked behind them. Its headlights went off, but its flasher kept turning. Sheriff Woodruff approached on the passenger's side and slipped into the back seat when Traveler unlocked the door.

"Too bad you didn't get the chance to meet Ernie Sorenson's wife," the sheriff said. "She delivered the Hickmans a baby boy an hour ago."

Moving gingerly, Traveler closed the glove box.

The sheriff grunted. "I thought I ought to warn you that

Cowdery Junction isn't big enough to have its own sheriff. When the need arises, they call me in. By then, of course, it's usually too late except for cleaning up the mess."

"Don't worry about us," Martin said.

"The Broadbents are a big family. They own one of the biggest farms in this part of the state." Woodruff grabbed the back of the front seat and pulled himself forward until Traveler could smell his peppermint breath. "I don't figure the two Broadbent boys would have much of a chance against a man like you. They're young enough yet, late-life arrivals but just farm boys when it comes right down to it. Then again, there's the daughter, Laverla, to reckon with. If it comes to a fight, her husband will side with Hubert and Lowell."

"What do you want from us?" Traveler said.

"Word about you two has already reached Cowdery Junction by now. Nobody's going to put you up for the night."

"It won't be the first time we've slept in the Jeep," Martin said. "We've got sleeping bags in the back."

"I've already called ahead and gotten you a room at the Cowdery Cottages." He opened the back door and stepped out, only to lean his head back inside the car immediately. "You keep that forty-five locked in the glove box. Otherwise, you'll answer to me."

Ten minutes later, the Jeep's headlights picked out Cowdery Junction's city-limit sign, population 1,445. A hundred yards beyond the marker, the narrow two-lane asphalt was blocked by a pair of pickup trucks, heavy-duty American models with oversize tires.

"Christ," Martin said. "I'm willing to bet you that sheriff knew about this all along."

The Jeep stopped fifty feet short of the trucks, close enough to see the gun racks in their rear windows. A pump shotgun leaned against the front bumper of each one.

The two men standing next to the shotguns were wearing

jeans, flannel shirts, and cowboy boots. They looked to be in their thirties and as heavy-duty as their trucks.

Martin banged his palm against the steering wheel. "Do we get out or make a run for it?"

"There's a ditch on either side of the road."

"I could back up?"

"They'd already be shooting if they meant to kill us," Traveler said. "You cover me from here while I get out and see what they want."

"At least you're faster on your feet than I am."

Traveler handed over the .45. "And you're a better shot."

"I'm getting too old for this." Martin cocked the pistol.

Traveler took a deep breath and eased out of the Cherokee, holding his hands well away from his body.

"Are you Moroni Traveler?" one of the men shouted.

Nodding, Traveler took a couple of steps toward the right-hand ditch.

"The said you were a big bastard and that we couldn't miss you."

"I take it you're Hubert and Lowell Broadbent?"

The brothers exchanged quick confirming glances.

"Are we going to keep yelling?" Traveler asked.

"Start walking. We'll meet you halfway."

Traveler didn't move until he was certain they weren't bringing along their shotguns. By the time they met in the middle of the narrow road, all three were squinting against opposing headlights.

"I'm Hubert," the taller man said. He was several inches shorter than Traveler, five-ten at the most.

Lowell was five-eight and heavier, about 175.

"The police tell us Mahlon's death wasn't your fault," Hubert went on.

"I didn't know him," Traveler said.

"Then why would he try to run you down?"

"You tell me."

Lowell shook his head. "Dad damn near collapsed when he got the news."

"Dad says he's never heard of you," Hubert said. "Neither have we."

"Maybe your brother was after someone else," Traveler said, not believing it.

"Mahlon didn't have any enemies," Lowell said. "None worth killing anyway."

"And you?" Traveler asked.

"We just wanted to get a look at you."

"So we'll recognize you next time," Hubert added.

"You didn't have to come armed for that."

"Our friends told us you didn't look like a man who'd listen otherwise. Seeing you, I don't understand Mahlon. He wasn't one to take chances. He never did anything without thinking it through."

Lowell nodded. "Our father's in Salt Lake right now making the funeral arrangements himself, so he can ride home with Mahlon. He's a frail old man. If anything happens to him because of this, we intend to hold you responsible."

"We're looking for a German prisoner who disappeared at the end of World War Two," Traveler said. "It had nothing to do with you."

Behind him, Traveler heard the Jeep's door open. He risked a glance. Martin was standing on the asphalt, his hands empty. The .45 was probably tucked against the small of his back.

"You don't look like father and son," Hubert said.

"I shrank with age," Martin called out to him.

Hubert started to smile then caught himself. He looked at his brother, who nodded. They both began backing up. When they reached their trucks, Lowell said, "Is it okay if we get our shotguns?"

"Just be careful," Martin said. "We don't want any more accidents."

One at a time, they picked up the guns by the barrel and gingerly stowed them inside their trucks before driving away.

Martin drew the .45 when they were out of sight. "They could have gotten themselves killed, or us."

"They're all bluff."

"Sure. Just like their big brother."

TWENTY-EIGHT

$\int$alina Road turned into Main Street as soon as it reached town. The Cowdery Cottages were a block east, on the corner of Brigham Street and Box Elder Avenue. The motel itself, a line of four stucco cubes, was half hidden behind a combination office and Flying A gas station now dispensing an independent brand of fuel. The station and cottages appeared to have been built as a unit, in the streamlined styling of 1930 art moderne, with glass-block walls, porthole windows, curved corners, and metal trim.

Traveler and his father were given the first cottage in line, the only one with a porch light. Traveler spent a restless night, listening to his father snore and waiting for the dawn. At first light, he bathed, flushing half a dozen shower spiders down the drain in the process. By the time Martin took his turn in the bathroom, Traveler had picked up a crude map of Cowdery Junction from the motel's office, explored the immediate neighborhood, and selected the Parowan Cafe for breakfast.

When they reached it, Martin hesitated out front, staring at the street sign and shaking his head. "We're standing on Broadbent Avenue, for Christ's sake."

"Are you hungry or not?"

Shrugging, Martin led the way inside. One of the locals moved over a stool so Traveler and his father could sit together at the counter.

"Our Saturday special is blueberry pancakes," the waitress said.

The small cafe, now standing room only, smelled of pancakes, coffee, and cigarettes, though no one appeared to be smoking.

"We make our own blueberry syrup," she added.

"Sold," Martin said.

The local who'd changed stools said, "You must be the ones the Broadbents are talking about."

Martin said, "They have to be important people to have a street named after them."

"There was a time."

The next local along the counter spoke up. "Old dogs can still bite if you cross them."

"The farm's only half the size it was," the first local put in.

"So is everything else around here."

The local on the other side of Martin leaned forward far enough to look Traveler in the face. "I hear Mahlon Broadbent got himself killed trying to run someone down in Salt Lake. Would that be you?"

"The man was a stranger to me," Traveler answered.

"Mahlon was a deep one, that's for sure, and a hothead. You never did know what he was thinking. His father's the same way."

Two platters stacked high with pancakes and whipped butter arrived, along with a pitcher of hot blueberry syrup.

Traveler spread the butter, added syrup, and asked, "Which way to the Broadbent farm?"

Both locals turned on their stools. One said, "Just follow Broadbent Avenue south until it takes a turn and runs out."

The main farmhouse, two stories of bleak metamorphic stone, dated from the 1860s, as did its near neighbor, a half-size replica. The larger house had a twentieth-century add-on front porch, with frilly cornices and railings made of lathe-turned spindles.

A hearse was parked in the gravel driveway. Half a dozen cars lined one side of Broadbent Avenue; a deep irrigation ditch ran along the other side, leaving only a single lane for the Jeep.

Martin had only one place to park, behind the hearse. Except for a parcel of fallow land directly across from the two houses, carefully cultivated fields flanked Broadbent Avenue as far as Traveler could see.

"My guess is," Martin said, expelling a long breath, "the closest mortuary is in Salina, so they're having a home viewing. We should come back later."

He was about to back up when a pickup truck parked behind the Jeep. A woman carrying a covered casserole dish got out and waved.

Sighing, Traveler eased his arm out of Doc Sorenson's sling and opened the car door.

"You go on in," she called to him. "I have to drop some food off for the widow next door."

Traveler watched her disappear into the smaller farmhouse.

"Let's get it over with," Martin said, starting up the stone walk.

Through the screen door, Traveler counted a dozen people all talking at once. He knocked but no one seemed to hear him. He was about to try again when a small girl appeared behind the screen. She sucked a thumb and stared at them.

"May we come in?" Martin asked her.

She nodded and ran off.

Traveler went first, ducking through the pioneer doorway, and was immediately confronted by a frail-looking man in a loose-fitting black suit.

"I'm Owen Broadbent," he said. "I don't have to ask who you are."

His sons, Lowell and Hubert, were watching from across the room. Traveler glimpsed a coffin standing on draped sawhorses in the next room.

"We're all family here," Broadbent said. "My sons and their wives, my daughter and her husband, my grandchildren, and Mahlon's widow." He sounded more sad than angry. "We all live on the farm. Mahlon next door, his right as my oldest, my other sons on Ellsworth Road on our southern boundary. The moment you crossed Mantua Creek a ways back, you were on Broadbent land. At this point, even Broadbent Avenue is private property."

"There were no signs," Martin said.

"The people around here don't have to be told," Broadbent answered.

"Are you asking us to leave?" Traveler asked.

He nodded at Traveler's sling. "If you want to sue, it's fine by me. My lawyer's Jess Moyle. Talk to him."

"We didn't know your son," Traveler said, "and we don't understand what happened."

"We're burying Mahlon at noon. Afterward, we'll be having friends in for something to eat. If you have anything else to say, you can join us then. Two o'clock."

"Maybe it would be better if we paid our respects at the funeral," Martin said.

A muscle pulsated in Broadbent's cheek. He took a step closer to Martin. "I can't keep you out of the cemetery, but my boys over there"—he nodded toward Lowell and Hubert—"they're both churchgoers and can recite the prophet, Brigham Young, as well as I. 'Behold, the sword of vengeance hangeth over you; and the time soon cometh that he avengeth the blood of the saints upon you, for he will suffer their cries no longer.' So my advice to you Travelers is to keep your distance. Besides which, my Mahlon would want only Saints burying him."

TWENTY-NINE

With Martin driving, the Travelers continued south on Richards Road, past a mile of grazing cattle and alfalfa fields, until the asphalt dead-ended into Ellsworth Road. There, they turned right and headed west. The farms in that direction were smaller, with houses every quarter of a mile or so. When the farms ran out a couple of miles later, the road began to wind up through a narrow canyon. From the top, they could see the Pavant Mountains in the distance, dominated by ten-thousand-foot Pioneer Peak.

Going downhill, Ellsworth Road turned into a single, unpaved lane.

Martin skidded the Cherokee to a stop. "Let me see that map."

The motel's handout featured the Cowdery Cottages well out of scale, along with small crude glyphs representing the Parowan Cafe, Pavant Feed and Seed, Higbee's Drug Store, and Fishlake Hardware.

"According to this, Ellsworth should take us right to the cemetery," Martin said.

"We've got more than an hour before the funeral."

"I want time to look for relatives," Martin said. "The Broadbents aren't going to be happy to see us, but I still want to take a look."

A hundred yards farther on, the road passed by an abandoned gypsum quarry. After that, the surface diminished into deep, uneven ruts.

Martin slipped the Jeep into four-wheel drive and stomped on the accelerator. At twenty miles an hour, the Cherokee sounded like it was shaking to pieces.

"I'm trading this in on something Japanese as soon as we get back to Salt Lake."

When they reached a railroad crossing sign, Martin stopped again to consult the map. "That's the old Denver and Rio Grande right of way. The cemetery should be over the next rise."

A four-foot iron fence with spear-point pickets surrounded Cowdery Junction's cemetery. A windowless caretaker's shed stood to one side of the double iron gates, which were barely wide enough to admit a hearse. There was no road as such leading into the graveyard, only tire tracks worn into the shaggy grass.

Martin parked across the street in front of a prewar bungalow where a small girl was playing ball with her dog. The moment Traveler stepped out of the Jeep, the dog, a black and white border collie, abandoned its ball and rushed to greet him, wagging its tail furiously. When he knelt to pat the animal, it collapsed onto its back, exposing its stomach for scratching.

"Janie doesn't like everybody," the child said.

"Is she named after you?"

"Don't be silly."

"What's your name?"

The girl clutched her ball and backed up a couple of steps. "I'm not supposed to say."

Her tone of voice brought the dog to its feet, snarling but under control. It moved between Traveler and the girl.

"She's a good protector," he said.

The girl retreated onto her front porch. She had to call the dog to join her.

Traveler and his father checked the caretaker's shed and found it empty. A hand-printed sign had been tacked to the weathered door: BROADBENT FUNERAL, NOON IN THE COTTON-WOOD GROVE SECTION.

The cemetery gates stood open.

"When we get there," Traveler said, "we'll stay in the trees."

"Keep an eye out for lost Travelers," Martin said as he started forward, head down, checking tombstones.

Traveler followed in his wake.

" 'I've paid my debt and so must you,' " Martin read off after they'd gone fifty yards or so.

"Just follow the tire tracks," Traveler said. "They ought to lead us to the cottonwoods."

Martin ambled along in the general direction of the tire marks, past rows of headstones facing east. He didn't stop until he reached a headstone inscribed with a finger pointing toward heaven. "Listen to this. 'As I am now, so you must be. Prepare for death and follow me.' "

Traveler was trying to get his father moving again, when he heard the sound of an approaching car. As soon as Traveler moved out of the tire tracks, a gray Pontiac sedan pulled alongside and stopped. Dr. Parley Sorenson got out, as did the woman with him.

"This is my mother," he said. "Ruth Sorenson. She wanted to meet you two."

She reminded Traveler of his mother, thin and energetic-looking, with black hair. In his mother's case, each gray hair had been plucked out the moment it appeared until finally she'd resorted to dye rather than risk baldness.

"How did you find us?" he asked.

Her smile accentuated a good sixty-five years of wrinkles.

■———■

"In a town this size, everybody knows where a pair like you are."

"When I hear things like that," Martin said, "I long for the good old days. When people knew their neighbors."

"The old days weren't what they're cracked up to be," she answered. "I ought to know. I'm old enough to remember them." She pointed a finger at Martin. "So are you."

He spread his hands, both denying and accepting her comment at the same time.

"I'd better go park the car before the others start arriving," Sorenson said.

"You go ahead," she told him. "We've got plenty of time to pay our respects."

As soon as the Pontiac disappeared around a stand of cedars, Ruth Sorenson started walking away. "We'll cut through the old section. It saves time when you're on foot."

Martin fell into step beside her. Traveler stayed close behind.

"I delivered a baby boy last night," she said. "Parley tried to get there in time to help, but he didn't make it. We're keeping count, my son and I. As of now, I've got a five-to-one delivery lead on him. Last night, though, I would have felt better if he'd been with me. Mrs. Hickman lost her first child, so this time around she had to stay in bed the last six weeks. Everything worked out in the end, and God showed His hand. A new life born to cancel out Mahlon Broadbent being called home."

She slowed to glance over her shoulder. "I don't blame you for what happened, young man. Mahlon was a wild one as a boy. He never did change much, though you'd think a man of fifty-six would know better than to try to run someone down."

"Tell us about him," Traveler said.

"He wasn't one of mine. I'm two years past retirement now, but I was too young for nursing when he came along. Some of the Broadbent grandchildren belong to me, though. Now, if you were asking about them . . ."

"Do you remember a German prisoner named Karl Falke?"

"My husband took a liking to you two, otherwise I wouldn't be here. Ernie's not one for strangers, though now that I see you for myself, I think he was right about you two. He said if I didn't help, you were the kind who keep stirring things up until they get what they want. Besides, Ernie figures it's probably a good thing finding that lost man. Maybe that's because Ernie was lost, too, when he came back from Germany."

She stopped at a tombstone whose inscription read, AL-BERT WILLEY, SERVED IN THE GREAT WAR. Like all the other headstones, Willey's marker faced east.

"I was like everybody else during the war," she said. "Germans were evil; they were the enemy. Even when I passed them working in the fields harvesting *our* crops I still thought of them that way. Then the shooting happened and the wounded started coming into the hospital. Seeing them then, I realized they were only young men in pain."

"Your husband originally thought Karl Falke was among the six from Cowdery Junction who died," Martin said.

"Those were hectic days. Government men were swarming all over the place, swearing everybody to secrecy. It was wasted effort as far as I could see. Nobody ever came around asking questions, not even the newspapers, until you showed up fifty years later. I can't see any reason to keep quiet now."

She knelt to pull a handful of weeds from around the gravestone. "There aren't any Willeys left around here to do it for him. Too bad he's not a Broadbent. They pride themselves in taking care of their graves."

Martin joined her. When the stone was neatly edged, the woman sprang to her feet. Martin groaned up after her.

"When the camp guards brought in those other six boys, they all had the same symptoms," she said once they were on the move again. "They had burning sensations in their stomachs, if I remember correctly. They were weak and nauseated. Their extremities were ice cold, their pulse rates very slow." She wet her lips. "Their tongues were brown. I remember that distinctly."

"You have an exceptional memory," Martin said.

"That's because I went over it with my son in the car on the way over here. He agrees with me, that it was probably some kind of poison. Old Doc Snow thought the same thing fifty years ago, for all the good it did him. He treated the symptoms. They seemed to get better. We got them up and out of bed and suddenly they were all dead. I've never seen anything like it before or since."

"You mentioned camp guards," Traveler said. "Does the name Maw mean anything to you?"

"You're in luck there. Old George Maw is still alive and kicking. You'll find him and his wife, Dottie, out on Talmage Road."

A magpie landed on a tombstone and squawked at them. A second bird took up the cry from the branch of a nearby sumac.

"All right," Martin called to the birds, "we're leaving."

"It's not us." She pointed out a gray striped cat that was crouched beneath a bushy dogwood.

"Salt Lake's too big for magpies these days," Martin said. "When I was a boy, I used to see them all the time. That cat better watch it or they'll pick him bald. You're lucky to live in a place like this, where nothing changes."

"Sometimes I feel the same way, but we're old, aren't we? Our young people, though, they don't stay. They head for the cities."

Martin took a deep breath. "You don't get fresh air like this in Salt Lake. It's times like now I envy my forefathers and the simple life they led."

She took Martin's arm. "When I catch myself saying things like that, I read the stones. Come on. I'll show you."

She changed direction and headed for a large Utah juniper tree. In the shade beneath it stood a double tombstone. On one side the inscription read HAROLD HILL, DIED 25 OCT. 1887, 1 DAY OLD. The other half said, EMMA HILL, DIED 8 NOV. 1887, 2 WEEKS OLD.

"Your memories of the bygone times are false," Ruth Sorenson said. "Life was harsh. There were no wonder drugs, no antibiotics. Half the people died in childhood."

She led the way around the double stone and showed them the verse on the other side.

> Gone before us
> Oh our children
> To the better land.
> Vainly wait we
> For others in
> Your places to stand.

"That's the great reminder," she said. "The good old days are only in our imagination."

"They won't work Sundays."

Martin grinned. "They will if I tell them it's one of Brigham Young's missing relatives."

"They won't believe you."

"Probably not. But they won't dare take the chance, either."

"We'd better make certain there isn't another explanation before you go running off to BYU."

"Mahlon came after us," Martin said. "That means he was anxious about something. This may be it."

They started back toward the car, following the tire tracks instead of Ruth Sorenson's shortcut. When they reached the cemetery's entrance, the gates were shut and padlocked. Traveler was about to help his father over the iron fence when Janie, the border collie, came charging across the street toward them, chasing a ball. The ball rolled under a gap at the bottom of the gate, hit a sprinkler, and careened away. The dog squeezed through the iron pickets, retrieved the ball, but tried to get out farther along the fence, at a point where chicken wire was covering a missing picket.

"Come, Janie," the little girl called from her front walk.

Janie dropped the ball and started digging frantically at the base of the chicken wire. The girl came running but stopped well short of the cemetery fence. Her proximity started the dog howling.

Traveler squatted down and patted his thigh. "Come on, girl."

The dog paid no attention.

"I think you can squeeze through the pickets and catch your dog," Martin told the girl.

She shook her head. "Ghosts."

"You're right."

Martin signaled to his son. They backed away from the fence until the girl felt safe enough to reach through the pickets and pull her dog out.

As soon as Janie and the girl had retreated to the sanctuary of their front porch, Traveler helped his father over the fence.

THIRTY-ONE

Traveler and Martin returned to the motel and asked the manager, a man named Frank Cheney, to put through a call to Sheriff Woodruff in Salina.

"It's the weekend," Cheney said. "It may take me a little while to find him. I'll ring your room as soon as I get through."

For a moment, Traveler considered looking for a pay phone, but then decided security didn't matter. Everybody in town already knew his business.

"We're in a hurry," Martin said and handed the man a ten-dollar bill.

The phone was ringing by the time they reached their room. As soon as Traveler picked it up, the sheriff said, "My friends know I don't like being called out on weekends."

"All we need is information." Traveler angled the phone away from his ear so his father could listen in.

Woodruff sighed. "Let's hear it."

Traveler explained about the two graves with a single headstone.

"You can't be sure someone's actually buried there," the sheriff said.

"That's why we're calling you."

"Shit. Stay right where you are. I'll get back to you."

Martin was filling the Jeep with gas from the Flying A pump out front when the sheriff called back. "I just got off the phone with Owen Broadbent. I didn't like bothering him on the day he's burying a son."

Traveler said nothing.

"The grave belongs to old Ethan Broadbent. He was killed in the Black Hawk War. The Indians probably ran off with his tombstone."

"There's been more than a hundred years to put up another stone."

"Owen's not a man to waste money."

"Do you believe him?" Traveler said.

"Owen Broadbent may not be as rich as he once was, but I don't want him for an enemy."

"What would you say if I wanted to pursue the matter?"

"Just keep my name out of it," the sheriff said and hung up.

Martin dropped Traveler in front of the Maw place on Talmage Road. They'd already driven to the Broadbent farm and back, checking the distance on the Jeep's odometer, 1.2 miles, a fifteen-minute walk.

Martin nodded at the thunderheads spilling over the Fishlake Mountains to the east. "You'll be on foot until I get back from the county seat."

"Maybe I can hitch a ride back to the motel after the wake."

"It might be a good idea if you kept the forty-five with you."

Traveler shook his head. "It's too big to hide."

"You couldn't hit anything anyway," Martin said and drove away.

Traveler waited for the dust to settle before starting up the front walk. The house wasn't more than ten years old, a tan brick cottage with two square picture windows flanking the front door. There was no porch to speak of, only three cement steps covered by an aluminum awning. The storm door had yet to be converted from glass winter panels to summer screens. Traveler rang the bell, heard nothing, and knocked on the glass.

After a moment, the inner door opened, revealing a man who didn't look old enough to have been a camp guard during World War II. His hair was thin enough, but his face was wrinkle-free except for deep grooves running from the base of each nostril to the curve of his chin. He was wearing a tan flannel shirt with military creases, tucked into tan trousers also sharply creased.

The moment he opened the storm door the smell of baking cookies came flooding out.

"I'm George Maw," he said, beckoning Traveler inside. "I've been wondering how long it would take you to get around to me."

The living room was no more than twelve by twelve, filled to capacity by an oversize sofa and two chairs. In the center sat a coffee table on which copies of the church magazine, *The Ensign,* were fanned out like a hand of cards. A bookcase designed for the set of encyclopedias that filled it was crammed behind the sofa.

"Ask our guest to sit down," a woman said from the kitchen, which was separated from the living room by an open archway.

"Take your pick."

The sofa's fabric crinkled under Traveler's weight.

"I'd offer you one of Melba's cookies, but she's baking them for the Broadbents' funeral feast."

"Now, Father," the woman called. "We can spare a few."

Traveler shook his head. "I'm going to the Broadbents myself. I'll sample them there."

"Business first, eh? I like that." Maw settled into a chair, then reached beneath it and pulled out a copy of the *Salt Lake Tribune*. The newspaper was already open to the classified ads. "It says here you're offering a reward for information about a German prisoner named Falke."

Traveler was surprised. Placing an ad in the paper had been routine, with no expectation of success.

"Just because we live in a small town," Maw said, "don't think we're yokels. I want the reward money up front or I don't say a word."

"If you'd called the telephone number in the newspaper," Traveler told him, "I'd have been here sooner."

"Why bother when everybody knows you're in town. How much are you offering?"

"Whatever's fair."

Maw tilted his head to one side as if listening for advice.

"You know what we decided on," the woman said, still out of Traveler's line of sight. "Stick to your guns, Father."

"I really shouldn't be talking to you. They swore us all to secrecy, you know."

"We could go to a hundred dollars," Traveler said.

"Do you have that much on you?"

Traveler nodded.

"Two hundred," Maw said.

Traveler counted that amount onto the coffee table next to the *Ensign*s.

Maw stared at it, licking his lips. "What the hell." He scooped up the bills and tucked them into the pocket of his flannel shirt. "The money's not really important, you understand, but I'll take it just to seal our bargain."

He leaned forward and lowered his voice. "Melba's been after me. You know how it is with women. Otherwise, I wouldn't ask a cent."

Maw's volume returned to normal. "It's done, Mother. You can bring out those cookies now."

The woman was tiny, no more than five feet tall, and so thin her bones showed. The cookie plate trembled in her hands.

"I'll leave you two men to discuss your business." She set the cookies on the table, then snatched the money from her husband's shirt pocket on her way back to the kitchen.

To avoid Traveler's stare, Maw tasted a cookie. "Oatmeal raisin, Melba's specialty."

He smacked his lips; his eyes continued to avoid Traveler. "The fact is," Maw said, "my conscience has been bothering me for years. When I saw your notice in the paper, I knew it was my last chance to get things off my chest."

He cast a furtive glance at Traveler before continuing. "First off, you ought to know I wasn't actually an army guard. I was a temporary deputy sheriff, since most everyone else had gone off to war." He thumped his right thigh. "My bad leg got me classified four-F.

"The army was shorthanded when it came to guards, what with the prisoners being spread all over heck and gone. Every farmer in the neighborhood was screaming for help. So I did my duty and volunteered to work overtime when I wasn't needed as a deputy. The extra pay was welcome, not that I wasn't entitled to it since everyone else was making money out of the war."

Sighing, Maw closed his eyes and touched his empty shirt pocket. "I was there when your man Falke tried to escape. I wasn't the one doing the shooting, though. I swear it."

Traveler leaned toward the old man, staring at him, willing him to open his eyes. When he did, he caught his breath and leaned back as far as the chair would allow.

He tried to answer Traveler's gaze but ended up staring at the table. "It happened right after those six men up and died. A bird colonel showed up and the shit really hit the fan. I remember him saying no one was going to believe Falke had been shot trying to escape, not when the war was already over. He practically accused the guards of murder. I guess that's why they hushed it up."

"That's the first I've heard of a second shooting," Traveler said.

"The official word was that your boy Falke escaped. They

made everybody sign papers swearing that's what happened."

Traveler didn't believe him, but could think of no reason the man would be lying.

"If you swore an oath once before," Traveler said, "how do I know you're telling the truth now?"

"What can they do to me at my age?"

"Where is Falke buried?" Traveler asked.

"I heard they sent his body back home."

"I don't think so."

"Are you calling me a liar in my own house?"

Not me, Traveler thought. But Major Lewis Stiles was and so was Falke's widow.

"You came to me," Maw said. "I didn't seek you out."

"I'm not going to stop looking just because you tell me he's dead."

"That's up to you."

"I ought to take the money back."

Maw grinned and shook his head. "You don't look like the kind of man who'd take money away from a woman."

Traveler stood up to leave.

"As long as you're on foot, you might as well ride over to the wake with us." Maw winked broadly. "No extra charge."

THIRTY-TWO

Traveler felt the sound before he heard it. It echoed in the chambers of his skull as swarms of vibrations teased the bones in the inner chamber of his ear. It set his teeth on edge and made him nervous to the bone. He hated the rolling drum of thunder. It always came too late to let him know that lightning had already struck.

He ducked his shoulders against the sudden rain. The dust raised by George Maw's passing car began settling onto Talmage Road. Mud caked to the soles of his shoes.

He took a deep breath. The singed air sent him to the south side of the road, well away from the northern line of box elders planted as a windbreak.

A quarter of a mile down the road Maw honked as if to remind Traveler that he still had a long way to walk. Traveler was heading east, almost directly into the squall line. The rainfall increased.

He put his head down and began jogging. By the time he reached the Broadbent house, he was soaking wet.

At the door, Hubert Broadbent handed him a towel before

introducing him to the fifteen or so men who were gathered in the parlor. Almost double that number of women were in the kitchen and on the back porch.

A long trestle table divided the dining room, separating the sexes, and was covered with casseroles, salads, Jell-O molds, and platters of fried chicken and sliced ham. A card table had been set up alongside to hold a large crystal punch bowl and glasses. There was also a metal tub filled with crushed ice and canned soft drinks, but no colas containing caffeine, which would have violated the Word of Wisdom.

The smaller children were assembled in front of the sideboard eyeing homemade cakes, pies, and cookies. Half a dozen older boys were taking turns cranking an ice-cream churn next to the refrigerator on the mud porch.

Traveler resisted the urge to join them, poured himself a cup of punch, and began circulating among the men. All were cordial, no doubt forewarned of his coming; they spoke to him of crops and cows and the weather. All the while, Traveler watched for an opportunity to speak alone with the family patriarch, Owen Broadbent. But the man never budged from his place in front of the massive rock fireplace that took up one end of the parlor.

The punch made Traveler so thirsty he lined up for a second cup. By the time his turn came at the punch bowl, the noise level in the house had risen considerably. He tasted the punch more carefully, suspecting that it had been spiked, but detected nothing stronger than fruit juice.

Even so, the drink warmed his stomach as he returned to the fireplace to stay within striking distance of Broadbent. Each time someone broke ranks to make a trip to the punch bowl, Traveler edged a little closer. Finally, he was leaning against the rocky shelf that served as a mantel, with only one man separating him from Broadbent. He was about to set his cup in a niche when he noticed two framed photographs. They were old and faded; they showed dead children. One of them, a girl laid out in her coffin, had half-open eyes and long, blackened fingernails.

"We remember our dead," Broadbent said as he drew Traveler toward him. "Even from the last century."

Rather than reply, Traveler finished his punch.

"It's made with homemade elderberry wine," Broadbent said. "I hope you don't mind."

"My mother used it for medicinal purposes. She said it's a lesser sin than some of the medicines that doctors prescribe," Traveler replied.

"I consider elderberry wine to be a sacrament at a raising feast like this. The prophet Joseph Smith agreed in his Doctrine and Covenants. 'It is expedient that the church meet together often to partake of bread and wine in the remembrance of the Lord Jesus.' "

Broadbent raised a hand to indicate the men around him. "We are the church, Mr. Traveler. We are gathered here to remember my son, Mahlon, who's with Jesus now."

Broadbent's gesture attracted his sons.

"There's a line-up for the lavatory," Hubert said, "and my back teeth are floating."

"I could feed the dog myself," Lowell added.

"We'll go out back," their father said. "We can talk better there anyway."

Lowell shook his head. "The women are out there now that it's stopped raining."

"It'll have to be the front yard, then," Broadbent said, "if that's all right with you, Mr. Traveler."

Once outside, Hubert and Lowell ran for the field across the street, charging through wildflowers and overgrown weeds until they disappeared from sight. The squall line had passed, leaving behind scattered clouds and shafts of sunlight.

Broadbent clicked his tongue. "To think they say us old men can't hold our water. Course elderberry wine is strong stuff to my boys. I was more than forty when the last of our boys came along. That's why they're still young enough to make fools of themselves.

The screen door opened and a woman joined them on the porch.

"This is my daughter, Laverla," Broadbent said. "Her married name's McKay."

She was a sturdy woman, in her fifties and nearly as tall as her brothers.

"Mahlon was my big brother," she said, shading her eyes to stare at the field across the road, where Hubert and Lowell were just now emerging from cover.

No one spoke again until the pair had returned to the porch and were perched on the railing. Then Broadbent said, "Mr. Traveler is looking for a German prisoner who disappeared, a man named Falke."

Laverla turned away from the sunlight. "I was only eight at the time, but I can still remember those prisoners working across the street, cleaning the cow shed and putting out hay. I used to watch them from right here on this porch. I didn't dare go any closer. If I had, Mom would have skinned me alive."

"You and your stories," Hubert said. "They don't change the fact that me and Lowell just peed in prime acreage."

"It's a damn shame to let those twenty acres stand idle any longer," Lowell added.

"You two clean up your language," their father said, "otherwise, you'll leave this house."

"Now, Dad," Laverla said, taking her father's arm. "This is Mahlon's day. Besides, we all know how you feel about Morag's field."

Broadbent broke free of his daughter and steered Traveler across the porch where they faced the smaller house next door. "I wanted to keep the Broadbent family together on Broadbent land. That's why I built these two houses side by side. One for me, one for my oldest son, Mahlon. His widow, Fern, locked herself inside right after the funeral. I built three more houses on my south boundary. That's where Lowell, Hubert, and Laverla live."

The screen door banged open and out shuffled an old man pushing an aluminum walker ahead of him. A teenage boy hovered behind as if waiting for the man to fall.

"This is my neighbor, Lamar Richards," Broadbent said for Traveler's benefit.

"I can speak for myself," the old man said. His right hand let go of the walker long enough to point at Traveler. "I own the largest farm in this part of the state. That gives me the right to ask what you're doing here."

"I'm looking for a missing person."

"They tell me you're named for our angel."

Traveler nodded.

"Did you change it, or is that the way you were baptized?"

"I'm a second-generation Moroni Traveler."

"Who's missing?"

"A World War Two prisoner named Karl Falke."

"Not even a Saint, then." Richards shuffled forward until he reached one of the porch chairs. With the teenager's help, he backed up far enough to sit down.

"You run along," Richards said to the boy. "Get yourself something to eat."

His helper looked glad to go.

"Does anybody remember Karl Falke?" Traveler asked.

Heads shook, all but Richards, who stared at Traveler in open appraisal.

"We were talking about Morag's field," Laverla said. "You remember her, don't you, Brother Richards? She was a prize cow, a huge black-and-white Holstein. When she got sick and died, Dad stopped raising dairy cattle and left her field fallow as a kind of monument."

Broadbent moved to the porch railing and stared out at Morag's field as if searching for his lost Holstein.

"It's a shame to see a field like that go to waste," Richards said.

"We've been saying the same thing," Lowell put in.

Broadbent shook his head. "I've told you before. It's not for sale."

———

"You haven't heard my latest price," Richards said.

"It doesn't matter."

"The way I hear it, you could use the money."

"I'll sell off everything else first."

Traveler took another look at the field. Twenty acres was a lot of ground to cover, but Cowdery Junction's cemetery might not be the only place worth looking for an unmarked grave.

"I could use a ride into town," he said.

Laverla turned to face him, squinting against the sun so hard a tear trickled down her powdered cheek. "I have an errand to run anyway."

THIRTY-THREE

Laverla drove a heavy-duty Ford pickup truck indistinguishable from those of her brothers. She ran through the gears forcefully, as if to discharge anger. Traveler fastened his safety belt as soon as she turned onto Broadbent Street and headed north. They were halfway to town, running parallel to freshly plowed fields, when she put the truck into a controlled skid that ended in a right turn onto Temple Road, a narrow unpaved track running east that looked unworthy of its street sign.

A few seconds later, the truck slid to a halt where the road ran out at the base of a small hill. Laverla switched off the engine and got out, leaving the truck door open, and began climbing along an overgrown path leading uphill. Traveler followed. The storm had passed to the west, leaving the ground damp and slippery. The only clouds visible were strung along the horizon where the sun was about to set.

"We call this our Hill Cumorah," Laverla said when they reached the top. "After the hill in New York where the Angel Moroni revealed the holy word to Joseph Smith."

To save breath, Traveler nodded.

"Cowdery Junction was going to build its own temple," she continued. "That was before our town began to shrink. Our young people moved away. Even my own children refused to stay on the farm. They're living in the big city now, up in Provo."

She lowered her head to stare at the ground around them. "There used to be a marker here and a garden, so people wouldn't forget our purpose. Now there's nothing but weeds. It was my mother who planted the garden. It was an act of faith, Mr. Traveler. You can see that by looking around. There's no water. She had to carry it here by hand. Sometimes she walked all the way from the farm with a bucket."

Laverla turned away from him to look down on Cowdery Junction. Viewed from the hilltop, the town reminded Traveler of a movie set, abandoned for the moment but still usable.

"Nothing's been the same since the war," she went on. "After that, the boom was over for us."

"It's the same in all the small towns," he said.

"Do you know what it means to be a temple town, Mr. Traveler? 'Saints would come here from all over to be married, to be sealed together for time and eternity.' Those were my mother's words. 'Laverla,' she'd say, 'when our temple is done, you go through a second ceremony for me. Give me a special baptism for the dead when I'm called home.' "

Laverla sighed. "I hate to think what she'd say if she were here now. I've broken faith with her, you can see that for yourself. That's why I brought you here, Mr. Traveler. To show you and to explain."

He said nothing while waiting for her to continue.

"My mother's maiden name was Helen Richards. She was Lamar Richards's only sister. When my father married her, a lot of people thought the two farms would be combined eventually. But after the war, the Broadbents didn't prosper the way the Richardses did.

"My mother knew she was dying that last time we came

■———■

here, just the two of us. 'You're my only girl,' she said, 'the one closest to me all these years.' I wasn't a child when she said that, Mr. Traveler. I was fifty years old. 'Promise me something,' she said. 'Anything,' I answered because I was terrified by the sight of death on her face.''

Blinking tears, Laverla watched the sun disappear into the clouds. The air turned abruptly cold.

"I never kept that promise, Mr. Traveler. Later on it seemed unimportant. But starting tomorrow I'll do it. I'll go to Salt Lake and put flowers on the graves of those young men who died here in Cowdery Junction.''

"Are you talking about the German prisoners?''

She nodded. "Once a month for as long as I can remember, my mother made a pilgrimage to the army cemetery in Salt Lake. She grew the flowers here especially. 'Temple flowers,' she called them, 'to honor the dead.' In winter when there weren't any blooms, she'd make wreaths out of evergreens and holly. It was a regular ritual. Sometimes my father would go with her, mostly not. But I always had to. Mother insisted. I hated that long trip as a child, losing a whole day away from my friends, when there were better things to do, or so I thought at the time.''

She fell silent. Traveler waited a long time before speaking. "Why did your mother take the flowers?''

"We had an argument when I was still a teenager. 'Those Germans were nothing but outsiders,' I told her. 'Nothing but Gentiles.' ''

Laverla rubbed her arms briskly, one after the other, as if trying to rekindle the heat of youth. "Mother looked at me and said, 'You haven't known pain yet, child. One day you'll understand.' ''

When she hugged herself against the growing cold, he took her by the elbow and began guiding her down the path while there was still light enough to see. She didn't speak again until they were in the truck with the heater running.

"I kept after Mother. 'Why do the flowers have to be taken to Fort Douglas?' I'd ask. 'Because,' she'd answer, 'it's something that has to be done. It's our duty.' Even when she was dying, I asked her to tell me her reasons. Do you know what she said? 'I don't want to burden my children's consciences with what I know.' Her very words. 'But never forget, those flowers must be laid down.' "

Laverla double-clutched the truck into gear, backed up carefully on the narrow road, and returned to Broadbent Avenue. There, she turned north as far as Wasatch Avenue, then left a block, and right again on Brigham. Three blocks later, she parked the pickup in front of the Cowdery Cottages Motel.

The moment the engine died she leaned back and closed her eyes. "You coming here, stirring up old memories, made me realize I've been making excuses for myself ever since Mother died. She was old and sick, I told myself, and didn't know what she was saying. Besides, I was too busy for such things, I kept telling myself. I had a husband and family to worry about. The dead didn't care if they got flowers or not. I even asked my husband, that's Ethan, what I should do. 'The dead weren't Saints,' he told me. 'They won't be raised from the dead.' "

She sighed. "I told myself he's right. If the dead aren't raised, they can't confront me when I'm called home. But my mother can."

"What does your father say about all this?" Traveler asked.

"It was an old argument between my parents. 'A monthly trip to Salt Lake is a waste of gasoline and time,' my father used to say. 'The chores around the farm come first.' That was one of the few times Mother would talk back to him. She'd shake her head like she did with us kids when we'd been bad, then put on her Sunday best. When she was ready, she'd go out and sit in the car and fold her hands, looking straight ahead, until my father would finally give in and do the driving."

"Why are you telling me this?"

"My mother was a wise woman, Mr. Traveler. She said it

was her duty to God to see to those men in unmarked graves up at Fort Douglas. It's my duty now. I think I knew it all along, only I wouldn't admit it to myself until you showed up and started asking questions."

"Did your brothers go along on the trips?"

"Sometimes, but my mother always said it was women's work. I was the one who helped her before I got married. After that, Mother had to go by herself much of the time."

"What did Mahlon think of the flowers?" Traveler said.

"You'd better ask Fern, his widow, because he never complained to me, not directly. He knew it would get back to Mother if he did."

THIRTY-FOUR

As soon as Laverla drove away, Traveler went into the motel's office and roused Frank Cheney, the manager, from his folding cot.

"I need a taxi," Traveler told him.

Rubbing his eyes, Cheney said, "There's no such thing in Cowdery Junction."

"A car rental, then."

"They might have one up the road in Salina. If not there, you'll have to go all the way to Gunnison."

"That must be twenty-five miles."

Cheney yawned. "I could close down the switchboard and drive you for a fee."

Traveler didn't like the idea of having a local with him. If need be, he could get around Cowdery Junction on foot when it was light. Even so, Traveler felt that the timing was right to visit Fern Broadbent.

"How much to take me to the Broadbent farm?" he said.

"I just saw Laverla drop you off out front."

"I didn't get a chance to pay my respects to the widow."

"Why didn't you say so? Mahlon was a friend of mine, though considering who you are, he'd want me to keep an eye on you and his lady. How's twenty dollars?"

Traveler shrugged acceptance.

Cheney snatched up the phone. "We'll leave as soon as Fern tells me she's receiving visitors."

The wake was over, the road empty of cars by the time Cheney reached the Broadbent houses. Lights showed in both, though only the smaller home, Mahlon's, had a porch light burning.

Fern Broadbent, wearing a work blouse, slacks, and running shoes without socks, opened the front door holding a drink in her hand and smelling of elderberry wine. She had that tanned, desiccated look fifty-year-old women achieve on tennis courts. Only in her case, Traveler suspected, it had come from too much hard work. Her eyes were red and swollen.

She ushered him into a living room filled with cardboard boxes. "If I pack all night," she said, "I'll be ready for the move tomorrow."

"Tomorrow's Sunday," Traveler reminded her.

"My father-in-law wouldn't spare anyone to help on a workday, not with Mahlon's chores piling up."

"I can give you a hand right now."

She shook her head. "I have to know what's in each box and mark it accordingly. If I don't, I won't know where anything is when it goes in the basement next door."

"Where are you going to live?"

"When I married Mahlon, nobody bothered telling me that the house goes to the oldest surviving son. That's Lowell now. You should have seen him here earlier, he and his wife, Thelma, measuring for curtains and furniture. They offered to help me move in the dark tonight, but I wouldn't let them. That's why I wasn't at the funeral feast earlier. I couldn't stand to see my sister-in-law gloat."

"I thought they had their own house on the other side of the farm" Traveler said.

"When Owen built his south compound, money was scarce. As a result, those houses are nothing but cracker boxes compared to this one."

"You'll be trading with Lowell, then?"

"I may be Mahlon's widow but I'm still only an in-law. If we'd had children it would be different. As it is, I'll be moving in with my father-in-law."

She saluted Traveler with her glass before drinking the last of her elderberry wine. "Tomorrow the widow turns into an unpaid housekeeper. My father-in-law will need all the help he can get, God knows, since there won't be much money coming in now that Mahlon's gone. It was my husband who ran this farm and made most of the decisions. Knowing Lowell, he'll run it into the ground, with Thelma's help, of course."

"Did your husband ever mention my name?" Traveler said.

She poured herself another glass of wine from an unlabeled bottle. "If you're wondering why he came after you, I don't know. Your name never came up between us. The first I ever heard of you was when Sheriff Woodruff drove down from Salina to break the news that Mahlon was dead."

Fern took a tissue from her pocket and blew her nose. "As to why he tried to kill you, God only knows. God or Owen Broadbent."

"Do you think it had something to do with the German I'm looking for?"

"I was five years old when the prisoners were here. Mahlon was ten."

Fern toppled a stack of boxes from a chair and sat down. Traveler settled onto the floor, keeping the spilled boxes between them so she'd feel less threatened.

"The war soured my husband," she said. "After that, he never liked anything German. Their cars were Krautmobiles as far as he was concerned and anyone who drove a Volkswagen was a Nazi. The German prisoners were to blame for ruining life here in Cowdery Junction, he told me once, though he never said why."

"Does the name Karl Falke mean anything to you?"

She finished her wine and set the glass on the nearest box. "I don't remember it."

Traveler rose and walked to one of the front windows, parting the curtain to look out. "There's fallow land across the street."

"Morag's field, you mean?"

"Laverla remembers seeing German prisoners working there."

Fern joined him at the window. "I remember the milk cows. I loved watching them. They looked so big, yet so peaceful, chewing their cuds and staring back at me with their soft brown eyes." She sighed. "Maybe the Broadbents got rid of them because Holstein sounds German."

Without turning his head, Traveler studied her reflection. "Did anything unusual happen on the day your husband came looking for me in Salt Lake?"

She leaned her forehead against the window, her breath misting the glass. "I don't see how it could make any difference now, so I might as well tell you. He got a phone call early in the morning and immediately went next door to talk to his father. They were at it for an hour at least. When Mahlon came back, he said he was going to Salt Lake to make sure the Germans didn't get another chance at us."

"What did he mean?"

"I asked his father the same thing at the funeral. He claimed he didn't know. If he doesn't, nobody does."

The woman turned to face him. She started to reach out but let her hand fall short at the last moment. "Tell me the truth. Was my husband driving drunk? Had he gone against the word?"

"The police said no."

"Lowell and Hubert blame you for his death, you know. They told me I should do the same."

"Do you?" he asked softly.

"I'll tell you the same thing I told them. Judging from the way Mahlon looked when he left here that morning, he would have run over anyone who got in his way."

She leaned so close he could smell her elderberry breath. "I guess the Germans have won after all."

THIRTY-FIVE

Traveler had just fallen asleep when the phone rang. He switched on the bedside lamp, a naked, shadeless bulb, squinted at the time, 12:05, and picked up the receiver.

"No calls after ten o'clock," Cheney, the motel manager, said. "Tell your father that I won't answer next time."

There was a click, followed by Martin saying, "We're in luck, Mo. The graveyard in Cowdery Junction is on the Pioneer Registry."

"You sound like you've been drinking," Traveler said.

"You know me. Whatever it takes to get the job done."

Traveler turned off the light but continued to see flashes of afterburn on his retinas.

"I've got two archaeologists coming down from BYU," Martin said. "We ought to be there in the morning sometime."

"It's hard to picture you drinking with members of Brigham Young University's faculty."

"They're practically foaming at the mouth at the prospect of finding a new pioneer grave. The cemetery in Cowdery

Junction actually marks the spot where members of the Mormon militia fell during the Black Hawk War."

"It could be Broadbent was telling the truth then, about his relative being killed by Indians. There's another spot we might look into, a place called Morag's field."

"Do you want me to run it by my archaeologists?" Martin asked.

"Let's see how it goes at the cemetery first."

The Mormon archaeologists, wearing white shirts and dress slacks, would have looked like missionaries if it hadn't been for their beards. They were both in their early thirties, with short, close-cropped hair and faces that glowed with the certainty of salvation.

When Martin introduced them, Thomas Evans and Leland Russell, they stopped pacing the perimeter of the Broadbents' burial tract long enough to shake hands. With them was Sheriff Woodruff, who'd come down from Salina after being notified of the pending disinterment.

"Saints shouldn't be disturbed," the sheriff said, glaring at Traveler.

"It's our duty to make certain that every member of the Mormon militia is accounted for," Evans said.

"You can be certain we won't make a move without proper authority," his partner added.

Both men were lean and tan and interchangeable except for hair color. Evans was blond, his beard red, while Russell had dark hair on his face and head.

"I forgot to tell you," Martin said for his son's benefit. "The church is sending us an observer. We won't be able to start until he gets here."

The archaeologists looked disgruntled at the thought of waiting, but didn't say so. Instead, they disappeared into the back of a panel truck with the BYU logo. When a Cadillac arrived a few minutes later, the pair reappeared wearing white overalls with blue BYU logos. There were two men in the front seat of the Cadillac, both wearing suits, ties, and dark glasses. They looked distinctly like church security as one kept watch while the other opened the rear door for their passenger.

"I'm Walter Clawson," the man announced immediately, shaking hands all around. He used a bishop's two-handed grip. When he reached Traveler, he held on long enough to say, "Willis Tanner asked me to give you a hand if possible. Of course, my first duty is to the dead, should we uncover an undocumented soul in need of baptism."

He turned to the archaeologists. "Your dispensation to work on Sunday comes directly from Mr. Tanner, speaking for the prophet."

They looked awestruck.

The look continued as they followed Traveler and his father to the site, where they went down on their hands and knees to mark off the area for digging. According to cemetery records, the fallen tombstone, Brigham Broadbent's, belonged to the indentation on the left, closest to the other members of the family. The imprint on the right wasn't recorded, except by word of mouth, as Ethan Broadbent.

Evans and Russell, after consultation with Clawson, decided to extend their area of search toward the cemetery's boundary line. Although the digging would take longer that way, they hoped to unearth artifacts from the Black Hawk War.

"How long do you expect to be digging?" Traveler asked.

"We ought to have the body uncovered before dark," Evans said. "As for the rest, it depends on what we find."

Traveler pulled his father out of earshot. "Church will be letting out in a few minutes. Once that happens, word of the digging will be all over town. It might be a good idea if I talked to Owen Broadbent before that happens."

"I'd come with you, but one of us has to be a graveside witness. We don't want any cover-ups."

THIRTY-SIX

Cowdery Junction's whitewashed oolite ward house took up an entire block in the center of town, bounded by Brigham Street and Broadbent Avenue, running north and south, and Parawon and Uintah avenues crossing east to west. A plaque near the front door said the church had been rebuilt in 1871 following the Black Hawk War.

While hymns were being sung inside, Traveler circled the building on foot, admiring its simple Greek Revival lines. By the time he'd reappeared from behind the building, Clawson's Cadillac was parked across the street. One of his men was watching from the driver's seat.

When the church doors opened a few minutes later, Owen Broadbent came out first as if he'd been expecting to find Traveler waiting. His sons emerged right behind him. But it was Broadbent who came down the walk alone, while Lowell and Hubert stayed behind, blocking the doorway and bottling up everyone else inside.

"Why don't we walk together," Broadbent said. "Just the two of us." Without waiting for an answer, he started west on Parawon.

As soon as Traveler fell into step beside him, the old man's sons left the church steps to follow at a discreet distance. Only then did the rest of the congregation begin spilling out. The Cadillac drove off in the direction of the cemetery.

"I'll be eighty in a couple more years," Broadbent said. "That was the age my father died. At the time, I remember thinking that eighty was ancient. Now that I'm nearly there, I don't feel much different than I ever did. How old do you feel, Traveler?"

Traveler shrugged.

"How old do you want to be?" Broadbent said.

"I always looked forward to being twenty-one."

Broadbent sighed, his shoulders slouched. "It's not right, a man outlasting his son. From father to son, that's the way it should be."

"My father says the same thing."

"They tell me his name is Moroni, too, but he doesn't use it."

"He goes by Martin."

"And you?"

"I was bigger than my father. The other kids soon stopped teasing me about my name."

Broadbent stopped walking to look Traveler in the face. "You're not a Saint, I know, but are you a believer?"

"The prophet told me once that all Moronis belong to him."

Broadbent smiled and started walking again. At the corner, he turned right on Main Street but immediately stopped to weigh himself on the scale in front of Higbee's Drug Store. The weight came with a fortune.

He read it out loud. " 'Today is a good day for investments. Act accordingly, but with caution.' What do you say to that, Moroni?"

"Caution is always a good idea."

Broadbent stepped off the scale and continued up Main, past the Rainbow Cafe, Tuttle's Dry Goods, Escalante Auto Supply, and Fishlake Hardware. At the corner of Main and

Box Elder Avenue, he paused in front of the Cowdery Theater. The doors were boarded up, as was the box office. Black plastic lettering on the marquee said CLOSED FOR REPAIRS.

"We haven't had our own movie show in town for years," Broadbent said. "These days you have to drive to a big city like Richfield to see one. Not that I've had the inclination. But it's a sign of the times, that's for sure."

He shook his head sadly. "Like I said, I don't think of myself as seventy-eight, but sometimes I get the feeling I've been working all my life just to reach old age."

He started walking again, more slowly this time. His sons stayed half a block back.

"Seventy years ago I lost two brothers to pneumonia. That left me alone to run the farm and take care of my parents when they got old. Then came Depression times. Hard, cruel times. I longed to get out of here and go to Salt Lake, but I knew my parents wouldn't be able to survive by themselves. So I stayed on. I married Helen. Together we took care of both our parents until they died. We never had enough money. We doctored them at home. We couldn't afford a hospital. Until the war started, we were land poor."

He stopped in front of the Cowdery Hotel, an abandoned two-story brick building whose south wall was covered with a fading painted advertisement: STUDEBAKER BUGGIES AND WAGONS.

"Try to understand, Moroni. I swore the same thing wouldn't happen to me. 'We'll have boys,' I told my wife. 'Enough to share the burden when we get old.' After we had Mahlon, twenty years went by until Lowell and Hubert came along. If they hadn't, I wouldn't have any sons now."

Broadbent nodded, then looked both ways before stepping out into the street. With Traveler at his side, he moved to the center of the intersection.

"Look at this town." Broadbent pointed down Main Street. "Do you know why things have changed? Why half our stores are boarded up? I'll tell you. It's because our children have moved away. They all want to get rich instead of carrying on family traditions that were good enough for their parents and grandparents. Getting by isn't good enough anymore. Everyone wants to live like they do on television."

He closed his eyes. After a moment he grew unsteady and reached out with one hand. Traveler caught him.

"You should have seen Cowdery Junction during the war," Broadbent went on. "We were a boom town. The government was buying our crops, everything we could raise. The only trouble was, we couldn't get farmhands. They were all off fighting the war. So we mobilized everybody we could, old men, women, schoolchildren. We even recruited from the Indian reservations. When we finally got prisoners of war, we thought it was a godsend.

"They were good workers, too, especially the Germans. Toward the end, though, they weren't getting enough food, what with the government reacting to the atrocities overseas. Without proper food, their work fell off, so us farmers took it upon ourselves to supplement their rations. My prisoners knew when they were well off. They didn't want to run off, despite it being a soldier's duty to escape."

Traveler looked for the man's sons and found them leaning against the aluminum siding that had been used to board up Prata's Lending Library. He was about to wave them over when he spotted a stone bench in front of the Cowdery National Bank across the street.

"Come on," Traveler said. "I need to sit down."

"City living ruins your stamina," Broadbent said before allowing himself to be helped across Main Street.

When they were seated and leaning against the bank's granite wall, Traveler said, "Tell me about the six Germans who died."

"I guess you know they were working for me, doing the milking and swamping out after the cows in Morag's field. When those boys took sick and died, my wife said, 'That land's cursed.' 'You're being a foolish woman,' I told her, but I let it go fallow just the same."

"What happened?"

"A farmer's a fool to get attached to his animals. That's why I should have known better about Morag, but we raised her, me and my Helen, when the calf's mother died. We hand-fed her with a baby bottle. My wife named her Morag and kept her in a pen outside the back door until she was old enough to take care of herself. These days, of course, it's easier to buy milk at the store than keep cows."

"Would you have any objection if we dug up Morag's field?"

"City people," Broadbent said with a snort. "Why the hell you'd want to do something like that, I don't know. But you're welcome to it. Maybe you'll dig out the devil and rid me of him once and for all."

Traveler studied the man. His face looked placid enough.

"We're already digging out in the cemetery," Traveler said.

The old man's jaw dropped open.

"We've got archaeologists from BYU looking for artifacts from the Black Hawk War," Traveler added.

Broadbent jerked to his feet. "Is that why the sheriff called me about old Ethan's grave?"

Traveler nodded.

Broadbent shook his fist at Traveler. His sons came running. Traveler turned to face them, keeping his back to the granite wall.

"They're digging up old Ethan," Broadbent shouted at them.

Lowell and Hubert skidded to a stop and looked bewildered.

"In our cemetery, you idiots. Now go get the car and come back here for me before they destroy our family."

THIRTY-SEVEN

The grave was open by the time Traveler returned to the cemetery. Owen Broadbent and his sons were there ahead of him. So was the Cadillac and its two church security men, who were busy roping off the area against a growing crowd of locals.

Gathered around the grave itself were Evans and Russell, the archaeologists, Walter Clawson representing the church, and Broadbent and his sons, along with Martin. Sheriff Woodruff was doing his best to disperse the crowd.

The body, what remained of it, hadn't been buried in a coffin but merely dumped into the ground.

"We're lucky the skull's intact," Russell said, kneeling in the grave.

"There's no sign of clothes," his partner added. "No matter how bad the soil conditions, there should be a belt buckle at least."

"How old is he?" Traveler asked.

"It's not a pioneer burial, if that's what you mean," Russell answered. "He would have been dressed. There would have been a coffin, something."

"They were fighting Indians," Evans said. "There might not have been time."

"Maybe the Indians took his clothes," Martin said.

The archaeologists exchanged looks. Russell said, "We don't think it's old enough to be a pioneer burial."

"You're wrong," Broadbent snapped. "That's Ethan Broadbent, right where he ought to be, next to my uncle Brigham."

Traveler nudged his father, who raised an eyebrow in return. They both knew that the archaeologists, deliberately or otherwise, were avoiding the obvious. The body was buried with its head to the east, its feet pointing west.

"A German prisoner went missing around here in 1945," Martin said. "If that's him, someone dug a hole for him."

The archaeologists perked up at the news.

"Didn't you hear my father?" Lowell Broadbent said.

"This is private property you're digging up," his brother, Hubert, added.

Clawson intervened. "If it means raising a soul, the church must give its blessing to this project."

Russell rose from the grave to face Martin. "You wouldn't have a picture of the missing man, would you?"

Martin handed him a copy of the prisoner identification card. "We can get you the original if you need it."

"Front and side views," he said for his partner's benefit. "Excellent."

Evans nodded. "We've been working with a new video-tape technique, superimposing skull images over actual photographs. It's helped identify war criminals like Josef Mengele. If need be, we can also have a sculptor reconstruct a face from the skull itself. That's expensive, though, and we haven't been authorized to pay for a sculptor."

Broadbent appealed to Clawson. "Check the temple records, Bishop. You'll find I arranged to have Ethan Broadbent raised myself. A full baptism for the dead."

Clawson glanced at the corpse and shook his head. " 'The trump of God shall sound both long and loud, and shall say to the sleeping nations: Ye saints arise and live; ye sinners stay and sleep until I shall call again.' "

"Now that you mention it," Evans said. "He's ass backwards."

Clawson glared at the archaeologist. "The grave is a holy place."

"Sorry. I only meant to point out that he's facing west."

Mormons were buried the other way around, so that they'd rise facing east when the final trumpet sounded.

"The Indians could have been playing tricks with our dead," the archaeologist added. "Look at his spine, for instance. It's been crushed. That could have been done by a tomahawk."

"Could it have happened during burial?" Clawson asked.

The archaeologists conferred with their eyes again. "It's possible," Evans said, "but only if they dropped him on a sharp rock, and I don't see one, do you?"

"Are you saying he was killed?" the church man asked.

"We deal in probabilities, and then only after our examination is complete. One thing's for sure. A man can't live with a spine crushed like that."

Broadbent whispered to his sons, who each took an arm and led him away from the excavation. Traveler watched them as far as Mahlon's grave, where Broadbent needed help to kneel on the fresh earth.

Clawson pointed a finger at the open grave. "I want this man identified as soon as possible. I'll authorize the hiring of a sculptor right now."

"If we're left alone to do our work," Evans replied, "we can get him out of here quickly and back to the lab."

"I've been ordered to pass on your findings to the prophet's office as soon as possible."

"We'll have something tomorrow morning."

Clawson turned his back on the archaeologists and shook Traveler's hand. "When you see Willis Tanner, tell him I'll be in touch."

With that, Clawson told his security men to stay with the

body and then drove the Cadillac away himself. As he was leaving, Laverla arrived in a pickup truck. When she got out, she was carrying two shotguns, which she gave to her brothers who were standing beside their prostrate father.

She glared at the Travelers. "I had to fight my way through a crowd to get here. Everybody knows what you've done to our family."

One after the other, Lowell and Hubert jacked shells into the chambers of their shotguns. The sound made Traveler clench his teeth.

"Wait!" Broadbent shouted.

He held out an arm toward Laverla. As soon as she'd helped him to his feet, the old man pointed a shaky finger first at Traveler and then his sons. "You stay away from this man. Do you understand me? His name is Moroni and he's a messenger from God."

THIRTY-EIGHT

Lael's BMW, accompanied as always by a gray sedan, was parked in front of the Cowdery Cottages Motel. She was tidying up the room when Traveler and Martin walked in. Willis Tanner was with her; he was standing in the bathroom doorway as if to stay out of harm's way.

The spreads on the twin beds had been tucked and tightened to military standards. Martin started to sit down on one of them, then veered away at the last moment, winked at his son, and settled into the room's only chair.

Smiling, Lael folded the towel she'd been using as a dustcloth and handed it to Tanner. He accepted it without comment and without moving. Until that moment, Traveler hadn't noticed Tanner's bad eye. For once it was wide open and almost twinkling.

Lael had traded her usual jeans and sweatshirt for a blouse and slit skirt. She eased onto the bed nearest the door and patted the bedspread to indicate that Traveler was to sit beside her.

He stayed where he was.

She turned toward Tanner. The movement opened her skirt, revealing a much fuller thigh than Traveler had expected. The rest of her looked full and lush, too, as if she'd made the transition from child to woman in the two days since Traveler had seen her.

"Maybe you should wait in the car," she said to Willis. "Please."

Smiling, he tossed the towel into the bathroom and left without a word.

Lael stared at Traveler while her hand stroked the bedspread beside her.

"Do you want me to leave, too?" Martin asked.

Without taking her eyes from Traveler, she nodded.

"I'll show Willis the sights." Martin carried his chair over between the beds, placed it facing Lael, and left the room.

"You'll have to sit by me now, Moroni."

Her perfume, Traveler noticed as soon as he got near her, was almond extract. He'd told her once it was his favorite.

When he sat on the chair, his knees touched hers. He tried to give himself more room but the bed behind him kept the back of the chair from budging. The effort started his shoulder aching.

She smiled at his discomfort. "What I have to say, Moroni, is so important I've already discussed it with the prophet."

"And Willis?"

"He knows about it."

"I'm listening."

"Did you and Martin look for the boy?"

The question surprised Traveler. "We have a client who's gravely ill. We couldn't take the time."

"I was telling you the truth, exactly what that Breen woman told me. Your son is in Milburn."

Rather than waste time denying kinship, he said, "We'll go after him as soon as we can."

"You'll need a wife when you find him."

"We'll need help, that's for sure."

■————————■

189

"You always do that," she said. "You evade the issue."

She leaned forward; her hands touched his knees momentarily, then retreated. The heat of her touch burned through his jeans.

"Answer me for once," she said. "Will you marry when you find him?"

"You're asking more than that."

"Yes."

"You're asking for a temple ceremony, for a sealing for time and eternity."

"That, too."

"You're asking for a conversion," Traveler said.

"I'm offering kinship with the prophet."

Traveler hesitated, weighing his response. In the end, he decided silence was safer.

"Is it true what Willis told me," she said, "that I look like Claire?"

"Your husband will be a lucky man. On many counts."

She sighed deeply. "But he won't be a man like you, is that what you're saying?"

"He'll be younger, closer to your own age."

Lael shook her head. "He's your age. That's one thing I'm certain about."

She stood up and kissed Traveler on the cheek. "I'll have a Moroni of my own one day and he'll be your namesake."

THIRTY-NINE

Traveler stood under the shower, massaging his sore shoulder until the hot water ran out. By then, he felt limber enough to make the pain bearable.

When he came out of the bathroom, Martin was stretched out on one of the motel's twin beds. "I prefer you with a sling on your arm, Mo. You're less likely to get in trouble that way."

"When people lie to me, I want to have both hands free."

Martin raised his head from the pillow. "We've got worse trouble than the locals acting up."

Traveler ignored the gleam in his father's eyes and concentrated on dressing—jeans, a heavy shirt, and work boots.

"You saw Lael for yourself," Martin went on. "It couldn't be more obvious."

"All right. I'll take the bait. What are you getting at?"

"You'd have to be blind not to see the way her clothes fit. That girl's put on weight. If you ask me, she's pregnant."

"Don't look at me," Traveler said.

"She didn't drive all the way to Cowdery Junction to see

an old coot like me." Martin scratched his head. "In a pinch, I suppose I could marry her. What the hell. The juices haven't dried up completely."

Rather than be diverted, Traveler said, "I wonder if the prophet knows she's been here."

"Willis drove her. He doesn't do anything unless Elton Woolley gives the nod." Martin snorted. "If Woolley nods in your direction, you'll be the one walking up the aisle, not me."

"Did you leave the pistol in the Jeep?"

Martin reached under his pillow and brought out the .45 automatic. "It's going to be dark in a few minutes. Why don't we wait until morning. I feel safer in sunshine."

"So does everybody else." Traveler went to the door and opened it. "Do you want to drive or should I?"

"Where are we going to start?"

"The Maw place."

Martin slid off the bed and handed his son the keys. "You're the one who knows the way."

George Maw opened the door and said, "I don't want you setting foot in my house, not after what you did to the Broadbents at the cemetery."

"Fine by me," Traveler said from the small concrete slab that served as a porch. "I can always have the sheriff come by and wake up the neighborhood flashing his red lights and sounding his siren."

Martin was standing two steps lower down, beyond the shelter of the aluminum porch awning. "That ought to thrill your neighbors and keep them talking for a long time."

"I haven't done anything," Maw said.

"We found a body," Traveler said.

"I heard it was old Ethan Broadbent."

"We don't think so. That's why the prophet has experts working on it at BYU," Traveler said, stretching a point.

"The prophet." Maw blinked. "I didn't know about that. All I heard was there wasn't much to identify."

"You know scientists these days. They can do miracles. It's my guess they'll be able to tell me it's Karl Falke by tomorrow morning."

"That has nothing to do with me."

"We already know his back was broken." Traveler stretched the point by adding, "That proves murder."

Maw backed away from the door. Traveler followed him inside; so did Martin.

"Mother!" Maw called.

"I'm drying the dishes," his wife answered from the kitchen but didn't show herself.

Keeping his eyes on Traveler, Maw retreated slowly, one hand feeling behind him for the sofa. The moment his fingers touched fabric, he collapsed with a grunt.

Traveler and his father sat on either side of the man, hemming him in.

"You told me Falke's body was sent home," Traveler said. "If he's buried in the cemetery, that means you lied. Or worse."

"I didn't kill him, if that's what you mean."

"Then why lie?"

"Mother," Maw said, an appeal.

His wife appeared in the archway, wiping her hands on a dish towel. Maw stared at her, then at the door. She shook her head. "Tell them the truth, old man."

Traveler left the sofa to take a facing chair, while his father put an arm around Maw's shoulder. Mrs. Maw stayed where she was.

Martin spoke gently. "We're not the police. All we're trying to do is help a man your age die in peace."

Maw stared at his wife for a long time. Finally, he sighed and started speaking. "When those six Krauts died, I never thought much of it. They were the enemy, after all. Then those high mucky-mucks, officers in their fancy uniforms, came down from Salt Lake and started looking for someone to blame. Everybody could see what they were up to. So us guards kept our mouths shut tight."

"Do you remember an officer named Lewis Stiles?" Martin asked, his arm still around the man.

Maw shook his head. "It was an officer who came here day before yesterday and put me up to this, telling you that Falke was dead and sent home."

"Who?" Martin patted the man's back.

"He walked in here big as life, acting like he was still my commanding officer, like he expected me to salute or something. He showed me your ad in the Salt Lake paper and told me what to say. Captain Goddamn Hansen, we used to call him."

"Grant Hansen?"

"Goddamn suits him better. I sure as hell didn't salute him; I made him pay through the nose."

"Did he give you a reason?"

"I asked him. 'Who's behind this?' I said. Do you know what he told me? 'I don't have any choice and neither do you.'"

Traveler said, "Hansen works for a man named Otto Klebe."

"Who's he, another goddamned officer?"

Absently, Traveler shook his head. Was Klebe involved, he wondered, or was Hansen trying to cover up for the army? Or himself?

"I'll tell you what," Martin said. "Let's stick closer to home. Tell us what you know about Owen Broadbent."

"A man starts talking about his neighbors, and pretty soon they're talking about him."

"Nobody's going to hear it from us."

Maw looked at his wife. "Rich people like the Broadbents take advantage," she said. "They've never done anything for the likes of us."

"All right," Maw said. "What do you want to know?"

"Tell us what it was like around here right after the war," Traveler said.

"My memory's not what it used to be, especially when it comes to names. But I can remember the old days well enough. I was working two jobs then, deputy sheriff and camp guard, to make ends meet. But your big farmers like Broadbent were cleaning up. Sugar was rationed, and he was planting every acre of land he could get his hands on in sugar beets. Always driving new cars, even back before the war, and then later those newfangled ones that disappeared."

"Kaiser-Frazers?" Traveler asked, remembering that Hansen's family had taken Klebe into their failing auto business.

"Those are the ones."

"A fool and his money," Mrs. Maw said.

"Mother's right. Sometime in the early fifties, he started selling off his land to make ends meet. The Broadbent place used to be twice as big as it is now. Of course, they weren't the only ones hurting when foreign sugar cane came back on the market. He switched crops and even got rid of his dairy herd, but too late. Old man Richards, though, he's as big now as Broadbent used to be. There's already a Richards Road and there's been talk of renaming Broadbent Avenue."

"Old man Richards must be ninety by now," Maw's wife said.

"Mother's right. But he still runs the place, with the help of his son and daughter-in-law, and they're no spring chickens either. Only last year Lamar was working his dairy right alongside his field hands until that stroke put him in a walker."

"I heard him offer to buy Morag's field," Traveler said.

"What did Owen say to that?"

"That it would be the last thing to go."

"I admire him for that," Maw said. "You take those sons of his, now. Mark my words. When they inherit the place, they'll sell out and take up city living before you can shake a stick."

"Why aren't they growing anything in Morag's field?" Martin asked.

"With Owen Broadbent, there's no telling. He's a stubborn man when he sets his mind to something. Maybe he's never forgiven Richards for taking away business. The Richards Dairy supplies milk to damn near everybody in this county. That why the old boy wants Morag's field. It backs right up against his prime pasture land."

FORTY

The church offices opened at nine in Salt Lake. Willis Tanner called the Cowdery Cottages at one minute after.

"You're lucky to catch us, Willis," Traveler told him. "We were on our way out to get milk."

"Lael told me what you said to her."

Traveler raised an eyebrow at his father, who mouthed back, "Don't trust him."

"I don't remember saying anything important," Traveler said.

"No games, Moroni."

"Tell me what you want, Willis."

"Was your answer to Lael final? I don't want you changing your mind at the last minute."

"What are we talking about?"

"Doctrine and Covenants, Mo. 'The unbelieving husband is sanctified by the wife.' "

"Take it from me, Willis. I'm a lost cause, beyond sanctification."

"You're not going to marry, then?"

"Is that you asking or the prophet?"

"You know how he feels about you and your father. His two Moronis."

"Tell him that his grandniece is safe from the likes of me."

"Amen," Tanner whispered.

"I have work to do, Willis."

"You are my work, Moroni. I've just had a report from BYU. We have a tentative video match on that skull. It's your prisoner of war, all right. As for his crushed spine, that's probably what killed him."

"Do they think it was murder?"

"Does it matter after fifty years?"

"What do you think, Willis?"

"I know you, Moroni. I can read you like I do our good book. 'I will take vengeance upon the wicked, for they will not repent; for the cup of mine indignation is full.' "

Traveler and Martin found Lamar Richards, who'd traded his aluminum walker for a motorized wheelchair, in one of his modern milking buildings.

"I used to get up in the dark to milk my cows," he told them. "I still rise with the sun to make sure things get done right around here."

Despite the smell of cow manure, the concrete building was immaculate. The concrete walkway on which they stood looked as if it had been hosed down within the last few minutes. A waist-high metal railing separated them from the cows in their milking stalls. Soft background music was coming from speakers placed high on the brick walls.

"I used to know my animals by sight," Richards went on. "Now I've got so many they have to have numbers tagged to their ears."

"I find the name Morag fascinating," Traveler said.

"She was a fine Holstein. I tried to buy her once from Owen Broadbent. That was early in the war, before things started turning around. Turning ugly, too, for that matter."

"Tell us about those days," Martin said.

Richards wheeled his chair around so that his back was to the railing. He locked the brakes and stared at them for several seconds. Finally, he said, "Most people won't take the time to listen to an old man's stories. Of course, you being detectives gives you incentive. You're getting paid to listen to the likes of me."

He rubbed his hands together in expectation of a captive audience. "The war years were good to me, good to Broadbent, too, for that matter. As long as the fighting lasted, we were raking in money growing sugar beets for the government. After the war, I invested in land for the future, for farming and for dairy cattle, while Broadbent opted for quick profit. I knew better, thanks to my father, who was a dairyman in the old country before joining up with Brigham Young. 'Son,' he'd say to me, 'buy land. It lasts forever.'

"Owen must know that too. He's no fool. No spendthrift either. But you don't look a gift horse in the mouth. When he came to me offering to sell off part of his land, I couldn't believe my luck. He must have been desperate, because he took my first offer, though I would have gone higher. Hell, look what I've offered for Morag's field over the years. Well over market value. The fact is, I never could understand his attitude, allowing good land like that to go to waste. If you ask me, it's a sin."

He released the brakes and pivoted his chair in a tight circle. "Look around you, for God's sake. Owen Broadbent could have had a dairy like this one. Instead, he gave up after Morag died. 'You can't fall in love with your livestock,' I told him. 'Not in this business.' But he wouldn't listen."

The old man leaned back and closed his eyes. Traveler waited out the silence.

Martin spoke finally. "Those six prisoners who died had been working in Morag's field?"

"It was bad luck, pure and simple. I had my share of POWs. It could have been them just as easily."

"Do you have any idea what killed them?" Traveler said.

Richards spread his hands. "They hushed it up, young fella. When I asked Owen about it, he told me it was none of my business. It was a sad thing, though, those young men dying that way after their war was already over."

"Some say they were poisoned."

"I heard that rumor."

"Their tongues turned brown," Traveler said, relating the symptoms provided by Nurse Sorenson. "They were nauseated and thirsty. Then they seemed to get better for a while and suddenly they were dead."

"Hell, son, that sounds like the milk sickness. I haven't seen it in sixty years. When I was a boy, we used to treat it with joe-pye weed and boneset, though that didn't stop it from killing most times."

"Are you saying they died from drinking milk?"

"Snakeroot causes it. It's like loco weed, only worse. No wonder Owen lost old Morag. Your cows feed on it, then they get the shakes and die. You drink their milk and the same thing happens to you. But like I say, the milk sickness has been long gone around here, so it's no wonder nobody recognized it for what it was."

The old man snorted. "That's what they get for trying to keep secrets, son. They should have come to me. If they had, I'd have told them what was wrong."

FORTY-ONE

As they neared Temple Road, Traveler pulled the Jeep onto the shoulder of Broadbent Avenue and switched off the engine. The sky was clear except for the usual thunderheads over the mountains. The temperature was somewhere in the seventies. The air smelled of growing things and hummed with insects.

Martin opened the glove box, flooding the Jeep with the stink of gun oil. He took out the .45, a trophy from his own wartime experiences, ejected the ammunition clip and examined it.

"I don't think we'll need it," Traveler said.

"Old men can be dangerous, too. I ought to know."

Traveler sighed. "All right. When we get to the Broadbents', you cover me while I do the talking."

"Don't I always?"

Traveler pulled back onto the asphalt and continued south on Broadbent until they came to the farm. They parked in front of the main house and got out. Traveler had been expecting pickup trucks with gun racks, but his father's Jeep was the only car in sight.

"It's a workday," Martin said, pulling out his shirttails to hide the .45. "The men are probably in the fields."

Mahlon's widow, Fern, answered their knock.

"We'd like to see your father-in-law," Traveler said.

The woman stepped out onto the porch. "I'd ask you in but the place is a wreck. I'm still unpacking. That's why Owen went for a walk. He couldn't stand the mess. You'd think a man his age would know better than to exercise on a full stomach."

Her hands went to the small of her back. "Here I am, my first day on the job, and I'm expected to cook not only for my father-in-law but for Lowell and Thelma, too."

Fern glared at the house next door. Traveler turned to see her sister-in-law watching them from a window.

"She's too busy to cook, what with making curtains and God knows what," Fern said. "But me, I'm a widowed housekeeper with time on my hands."

"Which way did your father-in-law go?" Martin asked.

"Do you think I have nothing better to do than keep track of his comings and goings? Why don't you ask Thelma? She's the one at the window all the time, spying instead of sewing."

Nodding, Martin started back down the front steps.

"If you must know," Fern called after him, "I saw my father-in-law walking toward Richards Road, though he still calls it the Broadbent Annex."

"Isn't that the back way to the cemetery?" Martin said.

She nodded before shading her eyes and staring west toward Richards Road. "I'll get the car out of the shed in a little while and go looking for him. If I neglected him, Mahlon would come back and haunt me."

"We'll save you the trouble," Traveler said.

"Make sure he's wearing his hat, what with the sun being so hot."

Traveler drove slowly, watching one side of the road while his father kept an eye on the other. They didn't catch up with Owen Broadbent for a couple of miles. By then, he was sitting on a fallen tree at the side of the road.

■———————■

"You wouldn't have something to drink, would you?" he asked the moment they stopped for him.

"Come on," Martin said. "We'll get you something back at the house."

Broadbent shook his head. "I'm going to the cemetery to talk to Mahlon."

Traveler got out and opened the rear door. "We'll save you the walk."

"I could have made it on my own, but it wouldn't be polite to turn down your offer."

When they reached the cemetery, Traveler drove through the open gates and followed the grassy tracks through the trees to the family's private burial ground. Broadbent bypassed his son's grave for the open hole the archaeologists had left behind.

"The way I feel now," he said, teetering on the lip, "they might as well keep that open for me. Better for everyone if I just fell in and they covered me up."

"A man ought to be buried next to his wife," Martin said.

"I don't know as she'd want me anymore."

"Women don't let go of men that easily."

"They're something, aren't they. They make up their mind to something and that's it. My Helen was that way. You couldn't cross her, not once she set herself to something. Like her temple flowers for the cemetery. That's what it's all about, isn't it?"

Before Traveler could answer, an engine revved in the distance. He knew it was a pickup truck even before it rounded the cottonwoods and came into sight. Lowell was driving; Hubert was sitting beside him. They both came out of the cab armed with twelve-gauge pump shotguns.

"Fern told us where to find you," Hubert shouted.

It wasn't clear if he was referring to his father or Traveler.

While Hubert spoke, Martin moved to one side, improving his angle of fire.

"Your sons are farmers," Traveler told Broadbent. "We're professionals."

"You heard me when I told them to leave you alone."

"I know about the milk sickness, so you'd better tell them again."

Head down, Broadbent plodded toward Mahlon's grave, stopping short to point at his wife's nearby headstone. His sons joined him.

"Your mother is watching everything we do here," Broadbent told them.

Martin moved again, continuing to improve his angle.

Broadbent read from the stone. " 'Disturb me not, nor my repose / Nor from my grave to take one rose. / But let them bloom and fade away / Like me, to bloom another day.' "

His sons exchanged quick looks.

"The guilt is not Moroni's," Broadbent added. "Wait for me in the truck."

They obviously didn't like it, but lowered their shotguns anyway, trudged back to the pickup, and reracked their weapons.

Traveler motioned to his father, who moved within earshot without giving up his field of fire.

"My sons are innocent," Broadbent said. "I want you to know that. That goes for Mahlon, too."

Traveler shrugged. "The war was a long time ago. They were only children."

"It's the old men like me who are cursed. We remember the past while everything else fades away. I thought about going to war, but farming was crucial to the war effort, so I was exempt. Maybe that's why I worked so hard, bringing in bumper crops. Then we ran out of manpower in 'forty-four and -five. On top of that, the prisoners they gave me didn't have the strength to do a full day's work. They weren't starved like those walking skeletons you saw in the newsreels, but they were weak just the same. Six of them, the ones in the worst shape, I assigned the easiest work, the dairy. I fed them extra and gave them fresh milk. Morag's milk. When they took sick, I didn't know what was wrong at first. Only when

■——————————■

204

they died did I remember stories my grandfather had told, that he'd lost half his family to the milk sickness back in the 1870s. In those days, they didn't know the cause, but in 1945 I knew the culprit, all right. Snakeroot. I guess I should have been on the lookout for it. Instead, it was one of my prisoners, that man Falke, who figured out what happened. He said he was going to report me."

Broadbent sank to the ground next to his wife's tombstone. His skin was ashen, his breathing ragged. Traveler knelt beside him while Martin kept his eyes on the pickup.

"I'm telling you this for one reason only," Broadbent said. "So that no one else in my family gets hurt. I want your promise on that."

"I'm not out for revenge," Traveler said.

"First off, you'd better know how things were back then. That machine-gunning in Salina had spooked everyone. The newspapers played it up. It was even on radio. Then, just when things started quieting down, those six up and died on me. My neighbors were so afraid the rest of the prisoners would escape they started carrying guns everywhere. You could feel the tension. I guess that's why I lost my head when Falke confronted me. We got into a fight in Morag's stall. The next thing I knew a board came loose in my hand and I hit him as hard as I could. Jesus, I can still hear the crack when it broke his back. Then he was lying there, staring at me, taking so damned long to die."

Broadbent twitched. The twitch became a tremor that started his hands shaking. He grabbed hold of his wife's headstone to steady himself. "I told the army Falke ran off. Now God's punished me. My son would still be alive if I'd told the truth. Poor Mahlon, he was the only one who knew what happened besides my wife. He was there during the fight. He was only eleven, but I told him he had to be a man. He had to be sworn to secrecy."

Broadbent touched his forehead to the stone. "Helen said we had to make amends. She raised her temple flowers and

I set aside Morag's field partly as an offering, partly because I was afraid the snakeroot would come back. But it wasn't enough."

He raised his right hand as if taking an oath. "In all the years since Karl Falke died, Mahlon never said a word about it, not to me, not to anyone. I'd hoped he'd forgotten about it.

"It's Otto Klebe I blame. He sent word that you were looking for Falke. That's when Mahlon went looking for you to protect me."

"Was Grant Hansen his messenger?"

Nodding, the old man grabbed hold of the tombstone and levered himself to his feet. "The rest isn't fit for Helen's ears."

With that, he moved on to Mahlon's grave, standing at the head where the stone would go eventually. "Klebe and Falke were close friends, close enough that Falke told Otto about the milk sickness before tackling me. I didn't know it at the time, of course. Not until years later when Klebe was taking out citizenship. He came visiting and said he needed money to start up in business. To meet his price, I had to sell off half of what I owned to old man Richards. The old bastard got a bargain, too, but I was in no position to dicker. I robbed my sons of half their heritage."

With the toe of one shoe, Broadbent smoothed out the fresh soil on his son's grave. "I know my boys. They're not going to let you take me off to jail without a fight."

"I was hired to find Karl Falke. That's what I've done."

"A man has to pay his debts. I know that now. Otherwise, someone else pays. Someone like Mahlon."

"Tell your sons to stay in the truck while my father and I leave."

Broadbent waved his sons away, and kept on waving until the truck drove off. He didn't speak again until the engine sound died away. "I'll be driving to Brigham City first thing tomorrow to collect my *loan* from Otto Klebe. It's about time he learned that his side lost the war. I'll give half of it to the church, that's a promise I made to Helen."

■————■

FORTY-TWO

Traveler and Martin checked out of the motel early the next morning and drove to Salina. They'd called ahead the night before. As promised, Sheriff Woodruff was waiting for them in his office.

He greeted them warily, like a man bracing himself for bad news. Two chairs were already set out in front of his battered desk.

Without a word, Traveler sat down to endorse Major Stiles's check for $132.07, the money that Karl Falke had coming to him.

"What am I supposed to do with this?" Woodruff said.

"Buy a tombstone for Falke once they decide where to rebury him."

"It'll cost a hell of a lot more than this."

"I have a feeling that someone in Cowdery Junction will pick up the rest."

"If they don't," Martin added, "send the bill to us."

Woodruff grunted. "I hope this means I've seen the last of you two."

"We're done with what we came to do."

"I kind of figured that out when Owen Broadbent dropped by last night and gave me something to hold for him. An envelope sealed and notarized, to be opened when he's been called home."

Woodruff shook his head. "Things like that shouldn't be necessary around here. If you two weren't already leaving, I'd run you out on my own."

After leaving the sheriff, Traveler and Martin drove as far as Provo, where they had an appointment at Brigham Young University's Department of Archaeology. Once they got there, Bishop Walter Clawson and his security men were sitting in for the archaeologists.

"I've had people working all night," Clawson announced. "You have a good friend in Willis Tanner. He called and gave the financial go-ahead. He said he owed you one."

Martin raised an eyebrow.

"Don't look at me," Traveler said. "I don't know what he's talking about."

"My archaeologists came up with a tentative identification, though they say they couldn't swear in court it was your man Falke." Clawson smiled. "Naturally, if Mr. Tanner insisted, I'm sure something could be arranged."

"It's a matter for our client," Martin said. "Not the legal system."

The bishop rubbed his hands together. "Good, good. Mr. Tanner told me you'd say that. I do have something you can show your client. My sculptor worked straight through the night to create an interesting likeness. Mind you, we didn't prejudice him by showing him your POW photograph. The result can't be moved yet, but I had a Polaroid taken of the head."

Clawson passed the photo to one of his security men, who handed it on to Traveler. The grainy black-and-white print reminded him of a pioneer daguerreotype.

"We'll show it to our client," Traveler said.

■━━━━━■

FORTY-THREE

The LDS Hospital stood high on the avenues overlooking the Salt Lake Valley. The expensive, private rooms had a view all the way to the Great Salt Lake. Lewis Stiles's small window looked out on D Street's Depression-era bungalows.

His son, Colonel Stiles, whispered in Traveler's ear. "We thought we'd lost him yesterday, but he rallied. 'I'm holding on,' he told me. 'I'm not letting go until Mr. Traveler gets here.'"

The old man's bed had been elevated slightly. His eyes were closed, his breathing labored; his gnarled, spotted hands lay on top of the flimsy hospital blanket.

"I owe you an apology," the colonel said. "I didn't really expect to see you again."

His father's eyelids fluttered. "Crank me up." His scratchy voice was barely audible.

While the colonel raised the bed, Traveler moved to the old man's side and took his hand.

"I knew you'd come," Stiles said. "You being named for an angel."

Using his free hand, Traveler removed the photograph and showed it to Stiles.

The old man sighed with relief. "That's him. Corporal Falke. He hasn't changed a bit. I'd know him anywhere."

He tightened his grip on Traveler's hand. "Did you give the corporal the money I owed him?"

"Everything's taken care of," Traveler said. "You can close your books now."

Stiles sighed and nodded at his son.

"My father wants you to have a bonus." The colonel handed Traveler a check for one thousand dollars.

Before Traveler could return it the old man was gone.

FORTY-FOUR

When Traveler left the hospital, the smell of spring rain was in the air despite a cloud-free sky. By the time he reached the Chester Building fifteen minutes later, thunderheads were spilling over the Wasatch Mountains.

Martin was in the lobby drinking coffee with Barney, Mad Bill, and Charlie.

Traveler accepted a cup. "It's time I talked to Willis."

"Do you want a witness?" his father asked.

"If I need one, I'm in trouble."

"Good. I feel like getting drunk."

"Charlie's way is best," Bill said.

The Indian fished out his medicine bag and nodded.

"Charlie's right," Bill added. "There's no hangover and no sin in his religion."

Traveler studied Bill's face, which was no longer swollen. "How's the tooth?"

"My dentist came through with a new crown, thanks to you, Moroni. Charlie's elixir is taking care of everything else."

Traveler left them spiking their coffee and took the elevator upstairs. Settled behind his desk, he called Willis Tanner's private number. A recorded female voice asked for an access code. "If you don't have one or if you have a rotary phone," she went on, "stay on the line and someone will help you." Traveler put his feet up and waited.

"Mo, I'm glad you called," Tanner said a moment later. His computer, Traveler knew, had registered the calling number and identified to whom it was listed. "I was just about to phone you myself. Why don't you and Martin come up to the office. We'll have some doughnuts and chat."

Traveler swiveled his chair to look out the rain-streaked window. "The temple view's better from here."

"Whatever you say."

Five minutes later, Tanner arrived wearing a raincoat and matching hat and carrying a soggy paper bag. He shed the coat and tore open the bag, revealing half a dozen doughnuts.

"Help yourself," he said, selecting a frosted one for himself.

Traveler moved his coffee cup to the center of the desk.

"I just got off the phone with your friend Cody Petersen at the *Tribune,*" Tanner said. "They're putting out a late-morning extra and wanted to give me a preview. What a tragedy, a member of the Council of Seventy being shot like that."

Traveler said nothing; he'd heard the news when he called Petersen from the hospital.

Tanner dunked his doughnut in Traveler's coffee.

"It has caffeine," Traveler said.

Tanner swallowed the evidence of his sin. "Before this happened, there'd been talk that Otto Klebe was in line to become an apostle. Why would a man like Owen Broadbent do that, shoot a bishop and then kill himself?"

"My client could have told you, but he's been called home."

"So I heard." Tanner snagged another doughnut and

dunked it to the hilt. "The trick is to get it in your mouth before it disintegrates."

"I need a favor," Traveler said.

Tanner finished his doughnut and smacked his lips. "Don't look so worried. I won't call it in. I owe you."

"What for?"

"We've been friends a long time, long enough for me to tell you how I feel about Lael. I've been in love with her for years, but she had her eye on you. So I stepped aside, but now that you're out of the running, she's come around. She's going to marry me."

"I'm happy for you."

"Now what can I do for you, Mo?"

"There's an old man who wants to be buried in the cemetery at Fort Douglas. He's getting ready to die and needs a plot."

"Haven't you ever heard of the separation of church and state? We have no say on federal land."

"Come on, Willis. All you have to do is pick up the phone and ask Washington for a favor."

"In the prophet's name, you mean?"

Traveler nodded. "His name is Jacob Decker. The only friends he has are buried up there, where he used to be caretaker."

"Consider it my wedding present to you, Mo. Naturally, Lael and I would like you to be our best man. Of course, you'd have to convert to the word. Soon, too, because we're planning a very short engagement."

"You wouldn't want to wait for me."

"A Gentile to the last, eh? I told Lael you'd say that, but we'll still name the first child after you. You're lucky I'm not the jealous type."

Tanner moved to the east-facing window. "Take a look at this, Mo."

Even in the rain, repair work was continuing on Brigham Young's monument at the head of Main Street.

Tanner reached into his suit coat and brought out an

envelope. "Here's your bill for damages to the prophet. We understand you've come into money, so the thousand dollars shouldn't be any trouble. Besides, there's no one else to pay. Think of it as the price you have to pay for being a Gentile in the promised land."